VOLUME **3**

ON THE PLANET OF TASTELESS PLEASURE

BILL, THE GALACTIC HERO

VOLUME 3

ON THE PLANET OF TASTELESS PLEASURE

HARRY HARRISON
AND DAVID BISCHOFF

Artwork by Michael W. Kaluta

A Byron Preiss Book

AVON BOOKS NEW YORK

BILL, THE GALACTIC HERO ON THE PLANET OF TASTELESS
PLEASURE (#3) is an original publication of Avon Books. This work
has never before appeared in book form. This work is a novel. Any
similarity to actual persons or events is purely concidental.

Special thanks to Nat Sobel, Henry Morrison, John Douglas, Shelley Frier,
David Keller, and Alice Alfonsi.

AVON BOOKS
A division of
The Hearst Corporation
105 Madison Avenue
New York, New York 10016

BILL, THE GALACTIC HERO ON THE PLANET OF TASTELESS
PLEASURE copyright © 1991 by Byron Preiss Visual Publications, Inc.
Introduction copyright © 1991 by Harry Harrison
Illustrations copyright © 1991 by Byron Preiss Visual Publications, Inc.
Published by arrangement with Byron Preiss Visual Publications, Inc.
Cover and book design by Alex Jay/Studio J.
Edited by David M. Harris
Front cover painting by Michael Wm. Kaluta and Steven Fastner
Library of Congress Catalog Card Number: 90-93197
ISBN: 0-380-75664-1

First Avon Books Printing: January 1991

AVON TRADEMARK REG. U.S. PAT. OFF. AND IN OTHER COUNTRIES, MARCA
REGISTRADA, HECHO EN U.S.A.

Printed in the U.S.A.

RA 10 9 8 7 6 5 4 3 2 1

To Joe and Ellen Donohue—
With Thanks

CHAPTER 1

DOCTOR D. PRESCRIBES!

TRUE, BILL NEVER REALIZED THAT SEX WAS
the cause of it all. But from time to time he had his
suspicions.

"It's a *satire*'s foot!" he roared at the doctor. "Well,
bowb-brains, it don't look so funny to me!"

Fortunately, Doctor Delazny was a civilian, or Bill's
military butt would have been Rotorootered. The doctor staggered back at the power of the Trooper's oratory
(and the onions he'd had for lunch), his eyes blinking
behind the bottle-bottom thick Exam-o glasses. "No,
Trooper. A *satyr's* foot. It's a creature of Greek mythology, a man-beast of rampant lusts who would cop-
ulate from dawn to dusk, and all night too as well."

Bill could sympathize. He was feeling pretty hard up

himself. When they sent him here to the Army Hospital on Colostomy IV they mentioned R and R. To any Trooper, R and R meant *Rutting* and *Rotgut*. Which of course implied the presence of a: human females, and b: large volumes of alcoholic beverages. Since the hospital had a nicely stocked bar down by its morgue, the latter was taken care of nicely. Unfortunately, though, all the nurses in this medical madhouse were steel robots. When he had groped back to life after his first heroic boozeup he had found himself groping one of them, which was a most unsatisfying, as well as rusty, occasion.

So now, here in the examination room, Bill was scratching his thinning hair with one of his two right hands, and staring down at his foot. It looked pretty repulsive.

"What is happening to it?" he whined.

"A good question," said Dr. Delazny. "I'm going to have to take a cell sample to confirm my suspicions ... But Trooper, what I think you have obtained is a hideous outer space infection which is a psychomutating plasmoid assemblage."

"Huh?"

"A mood foot."

"It's his fault, his fault, that bowbing Chinger spy, Eager Beager. Ever since he did me the big favor of replacing my giant chicken foot I have had nothing but foot trouble."

Bill clamped his mouth shut, knowing that no good could come of talking about his Chinger encounter. The Chinger spy was nothing but trouble, trying to make him promise to give up war! Betray the Empire! Sow dissension and peace-talk. Plant propaganda. Work toward disarmament and a treaty between Humans and Chingers. Of course, Bill could never betray his fierce loyalty to the Imperial Troopers, as much as he would like to, since his brain was far too sodden with conditioning drugs and behavioral neuro-plants for that.

As soon as he'd gotten back to headquarters, he'd squawked. The Brass was so grateful for the poop on Chinger mentality after he'd been debriefed, when his foot started getting weird, they sent him out to this planet for treatment by a specialist in procto–podiatry, Dr. Latex Delazny.

"Yes, it conforms with neural–image forms generated by the synthesis of neo–cortex and F–complex relationships. In other words, Trooper, your foot thinks it's stuck on the body of a creature who thinks about nothing but sex and drinking." He smiled grimly and shook his head. "Now, does that bear a resemblance to anyone you're familiar with?"

Dr. Delazny had a highly specialized medical education with higher degrees in eye–ear–nose–and–throat plus a much lower degree in proctology. In other words, he was a specialist in mouths and arseholes, which meant that he treated a lot of lawyers—doing an excellent business in transplants since with lawyers the two were interchangeable. However, when the Emperor, in a sudden mood of sadistic philanthropy, had executed all of the lawyers in the Known Universe, Dr. Delazny found his practice extinguished and had to find work elsewhere. He'd confided all this to Bill the other night in the bar over a bottle of Old Granbowb.

"Damn, Doc. A man's gotta do what a man's gotta do. Drink. How else can a Trooper stay sane in this criminally insane outfit? And a man needs the comforts that only a woman can bring!" Bill sniveled with self pity, then sighed passionately as he thought about all his old girlfriends. And the young ones as well. His battle–hardened musculature tensed as he thought about Meta, shipped out now to some godforsaken strife–torn planet, fighting in this hellish but glorious Chinger conflict. Meta! Now there was a *woman*! Those eyes! That chest! That tight, rounded rear end that put Inga–Maria Calyphigia's, back on Phigerinadon II, to shame! But then, Meta was hardly the type of woman who would plant bare feet in a kitchen and produce babies for the rest of her life. Meta was the kind of gal Bill's mother had warned him about—mentally, physically, emotionally his superior, with a sex drive that could power a starship, once she got it in gear. And just as they'd gotten their relationship over the first hump, so to speak, the bowbing Troopers had to detail her somewhere else. Bowb and double bowb!

Bill wondered if there was something going wrong with him. Had the Troopers left a shred of dignity and humanity in his body? It didn't seem possible. Was he capable of love? Did he even know how to spell the word? Was that what he was looking for? Was that why he was so restless of late? Was that why he'd started smuggling TRUE SLUSHY SPACE ROMANCE comix inside the copies of BLOOD PORN SPLATTER TALES that the recruits saw him reading?

Naw. What good was a regular woman, anyway? Like the Troopers said, a woman would make him stop smoking, drinking to excess, swearing incontinently while lusting after anything female that strolled by— and weren't those the vital ingredients that life was really all about?

Dr. Latex Delazny looked down again at the readout from the computer. "Fascinating. Tell me Bill, do you know anything about the endocrine system?"

"Isn't that the swamp and poison ocean worlds over by the Cassiopeian system?"

Doctor Delazny scratched angrily at the scruff on his balding head. He looked to be a man in his late thirties, fine spiderwebs of wrinkles, as well as fine spiders, just starting to radiate from his eyes. He was thin and distracted-seeming, as though his mind operated like a three ring circus, and he was far more interested in the acrobatic act in the center than this clown act before him.

"No, you military moron. I'm talking about human physiology. The endocrine system, the pituitary, the thyroid, the adrenals...etcetera, etcetera. And of course, the sex glands. Human anatomy, sod-head! Don't they teach you that in the Troopers?"

Bill shook his head in humble contrition.

"Important bodily functions, Bill. Particularly the sex glands. Did you know I have a PhD in endocrinology? But do you think the Empire has any use for that? Bah. Feet and sphincters, sphincters and feet. That's all they want me to work on. What a dreadful waste."

He was a tall, gangling scarecrow, looking as though he slept in his lab coat, which happened pretty often anyway. But he still had certain strengths. Bill was particularly impressed by the way the doctor had been able to put away Antarean Alkpee in the bar the other night.

Doctor Delazny mused boredly over the readouts on the table. "My goodness, Bill, talking about secretion, your lower ductless glands seem particularly active. Most interesting, Trooper—you seem to have enough testosterone in your body to grow a beard on an elephant!"

Delazny peered at Bill appraisingly, and the Trooper felt suddenly uncomfortable at being moved to center stage.

"What about my foot, Doc? Remember, that's what I came in about."

Doctor Delazny cleared his throat, puffed out his chest and spoke out authoritatively.

"Trooper, what I'm prescribing for the time being is that you spend your sacktime and rectime here at the hospital. Walk on the polluted beach, visit the garbage dump, tour the factory down the road...Rest! Relax! Avail yourself of the recreational facilities we have here at Grin N' Clinic! This will give me the opportunity to examine the cellular composition of your foot."

"You're not going to give me a *new* one?"

"I would love to, Bill, but haven't you got it through that thick farm-bred and alcohol-preserved skull of yours? This army has a foot shortage!"

"Shoulda never gone on the metric system!" grumbled Bill. The latrine rumor mill had leaked the story. Used to be, Army Medics had lots of feet in freezers, but when the order came down from Helior for the Army to go metric, the noncoms hadn't understood. "Get rid of the feet!" the officers had yowled. And so the noncoms had dumped the frozen feet.

Bill pulled on a sweatsock over his cloven hoof, then covered that with a boot. He looked down nostalgically at the scuffed footwear, remembering the shine that Eager Beager used to be able to raise on his issue Trooper boots, back when Bgr the Chinger was hiding out in a robot disguised as a recruit slogging through training camp. He'd never had such good-looking boots since.

"Maybe you're right, Doc. Maybe I could use some rest. Drink less, plenty of fresh air and raw fruit." It sounded positively repulsive. But he let this decaying sawbones think he was going along with the plan until he came up with a plan to find a way out of here.

Ahh, but how little did Trooper Bill realize it, but "rest" was not precisely a commodity penciled into his particular cosmic itinerary for the next week. If only the Doctor had not suggested a walk along the beach, then perhaps Bill's mind-blowing, super-exciting and absolutely page-turning adventure amongst the myths and Gods, to say nothing of the incredible Over-Gland, would never have occurred.

"Oh, and Bill—about those hemorrhoids that we don't have the right medicine for?" said Doc Delazny as Bill started walking away through the maze of hi-tech medical machinery.

"Yeah?" said Bill turning around, his posterior tingling hopefully.

"Dear fellow, I'm afraid that you are just going to have to sit this batch out!"

Bill called the quack something so revolting that it instantly cheered him up, then stalked back to the bar. It was Happy Hour and it was a Monday, which meant that they were giving out free pickled porkuswine feet hors d'oeuvres, one of Bill's favorites.

He just hoped they didn't give his "mood foot" the wrong idea.

CHAPTER 2

READING MATTER

BILL DREAMED.

He dreamed that he was a farmer again, sweating behind a robo-mule. He dreamed that his prime ambition, his only ambition, in life was to become a Technical Fertilizer Operator. Some said that it was a crappy job—but not he! Smiling in his sleep he dreamed of going forth and spreading mounds of fragrant manure upon the gentle plains of the planets of the galaxy, rising up high and noisome, the fragrant delight of the magic scent tingling the nascent nostrils of a billion happy farmers.

Then the dream changed and Deathwish Drang came to him, fluttering gently on gossamer angel's wings.

"Trideo Games, Bill!" he chuckled and twanged a

fang. "Your future is Trideo Games!"

Now Bill was very young in his dream, for as a little boy he had always yearned to play Trideo in town with the other kids, and he always beat them, yes he did, but only in his fevered imagination. For of course he never went to town, had no money either: Trideo was just the stuff of dreams. So when Deathwish Drang's proclamation filtered through the magnificent fangs of his, Bill thought, Yes! It's true! When Drang unfurled the sparkling contract in front of his eyes, the contract to become a hot-shot Trideo game contestant amongst the myriad civilized worlds of the galaxy, Bill signed without hesitation.

Trideo Games involved not only hand-eye reflexes and keen nerves, but mental coordination as well. The player was strapped securely into a machine that was a tin and plastic imitation of a spaceship, complete with fake lasers and ersatz pulsar torpedoes, etiolated tractor and pulsar beams, and all that good old docsmith stuff. Then, using a tridee screen, the contestant fought the chicken Chingers in their horrible dreadful Deathships from Sewer-Hell.

In his dream, the Chingers were again seven-foot monsters with razor-sharp teeth, rumored to snack on toasted human babies while watching television from their Slime-Couches. "Death to the Chingers," he howled as he arced through their armadas, defying the laws of physics as he nailed Chinger hate-ships with noble zaps of his powerful beamers.

But then, in his dream, a Chinger destroyer-boat caught him broadside and tore a hole through the side of the Trideo machine. Bill was stunned. This was just a game! How could... Then he realized. He'd been a patsy! The Empire had tricked him. He really *was* fighting a real war!

It wasn't just a game.

Then hundreds of seven-inch tall Chingers swarmed through the rent, each of them armed with a seven-foot tall cutlass. Which seemed kind of impossible—but who asks questions in dreams?

He was *doomed*!

Bill woke up. His head felt like it was splitting open and his sinuses were on fire.

Damned book!

Goddamn cheap stripped hospital book!

His throbbing nasal passages felt as though mad scientists had filled them full with acid. He stumbled out of bed to the sink, held his head and moaned and tried to blow his nose at the same time. The pain increased, that was all. Groaning, he tried once again. Taking a deep breath sounding his horn.

"Kaaa-CHOO!" said Bill, clutching the pseudo-porcelain rim.

With an elephantine blast of his nose bugle an inch-long lozenge shot out, fitted with rubber appendages whose metal tips sparked fitfully as it bounced into the sink and hopped and fizzled about until he turned on the water and the thing spattered into extinction.

The book.

It was labeled, in raised letters, FENDER BENDER by Orson Bean Curd. Bill remembered faintly that it was about an idiot-savant servo-mechanic hijacked by Chingers and fiendishly used against the noble Empire, but nothing much more, since he'd only managed to get the book halfway up his nose. "Don't forget to sniff out the exciting sequel, MACARONI OF THE MORONS, coming soon from Mace Books!" read another smaller label, only slightly smeared with nose gunk.

With the high rate of illiteracy amongst the pioneer worlds, book companies had begun to market these "Stick-a-Books" with great success. They came with their own automatic "lit-pack": engrams that tendrilled into the user's brain and programmed the unhappy reader with the words and concepts necessary to understand the book. Then, when the victim had finished "reading" the little machine's contents, it would puff out sneezing powder. The theory was that a quick blast of sneezing would shoot the infernal gadget out. After a quick rinse, it was ready for another consumer! However, due to the capitalistic process of distribution, and the infamous Rack-Space Wars (a space conflict that even chilled Bill's veteran bones) the practice of "stripping" was used on these books, rather than going to the expense of shipping the full product back to the publisher. This involved tearing out a tab of circuitry imbued with identification properties which gave retailers credit for the product. Retailers then sold the remainder at reduced rates to the military and planets for the mentally retarded. Unfortunately, much of the guts of the book itself was also stripped in the process, so that chances were if you were a hospital patient and you tried to read one of these "special editions" as they were euphemistically labeled, you only got part of the book.

Such was the case, clearly, with the one that Bill had stuffed up his nostril last night, meaning to read for a while before turning in. Not only that, but apparently the bowby thing hadn't been properly cleaned after it had last been used and had the definite sniff of someone else's sinus!

Bill finished blowing his tortured nose while his eyes streamed with tears, and then went to the side of his bed for a swig of Pepto Abysmal—The Calming Internal Antiseptic and Nose Purifier! This cheap, rotten, godforsaken hospital was getting on his nerves. Not only were the beginnings or ends of their books lopped off, but the sanitary conditions weren't much better than back at Camp Leon Trotsky where he'd done his boot training. Colostomy IV, a planet only recently discovered, though it had a reasonable oxygen content to its atmosphere soup (along with curious trace amounts of incense and airborne alkaloids; scientific speculation posited a dead, lost race of either Buddhists, Hindus or hippies) and it swung around a GO-GO star (very close to Sol in type), absolutely no living intelligent beings had been discovered upon its surface. Just lots of floral land undergoing the usual geological hiccups—and lots of mysterious dark ocean. Since the planet happened to be somewhere between somewhere and somewhere else, both somewheres being equally repulsive, the Troopers had naturally chosen to build a transient camp, reppel depple, Senior Officers Whorehouse and this hospital here, on the shores of the great black ocean, tideless and ominous. They also built a water dehydration plant on the shore to ship out powdered water for the troopers (just add water . . . voila! Water!)

Bill chased the chalky medicine with a glass of foul-tasting water and went back to bed. He dozed intermittently, but as rosy-fingered dawn fingered the window sill while pain fingered his frontal lobes he was still feeling relatively sleepless. His headache had abated somewhat, but his mood foot felt weird. It was all tingly, like it was just waking out of leg-sleep. Maybe, he thought, he should go to see Dr. Delazny about this immediately. It felt like Tinkerbell had just jammed her wand up his cloven hoof, and all kinds of aerie fairie nonsense was happening inside!

Bill put on his torn, five-ply paper robe and moaned his way out of the ward, hoping to wake up the four doped-to-the-gills Troopers he shared it with. No such luck. The sick bowbs were sleeping, if not the sleep of the innocent, then at least the sleep of the narcoleptic.

He went down to the Doc's office, in the basement, conveniently situated by the bar and the morgue (many of Doctor Delazny's patients were victims of the dreaded Pedosphincter Rot, a wildly metastasizing mutant xenocancer killing Troopers by the platoon, whose distant ancestor was athlete's foot, and that struck the nether regions of the human body. Hence his dual specialty. And also hence his proximity to the morgue.) By now Bill's foot felt as though sparklers were pixilating in his heel!

As the lift banged to an abrupt halt on Level Zero and the doors wheezed open, Bill thought he caught a sight of Doctor Delazny's balding dome disappearing into the laundry room, followed by the flapping tails of his lab coat.

What was he in such a hurry for?

And why was he running into the *laundry* room?

"Hey Doc!" he cried, limping along, cringing with the odd sensations that kept shooting up his leg. "Wait up! I got to talk to you!"

He pushed open the swinging doors marked "Laundry." The room was lined with shelves of linens, amongst which scurried ratfinks—native rodent-like creatures who swarmed the Trooper installations and appeared to feed on linoleum wax and toenail parings. In the middle of the room, a laundry chute depended from the ceiling, beneath which a small basket of soiled towels, garments and sheets breathed up stale human body odors.

"Doc! Doc Delazny?" Bill stepped in, looking around. A pair of filthy trousers zoomed down the chute and landed atop his head. He snarled and threw it at a clump of copulating ratfinks, who proceeded to devour it.

No sign of the Doctor. But Bill could have sworn—

Oh well. Bill left and checked Doc Delazny's examination room. Nobody.

A bright orange and blue neon sign blasted out the letters HOSPITAL BAR just as brightly as ever, but the door was locked. It was closed. It didn't open till 0630 hours. The authorities here were vaguely considering keeping a 24-hour bartender, but hadn't got around to it yet. The morgue was deserted—except of course for the dead people. There was only one other room that Doctor Delazny could have gone down here, though Bill was loath to venture there. It was a gilt door set with fake diamonds and labeled proudly "Heroes' Haven—Only the Best Damn Troopers in the Galaxy Enter Here." He cringed back, the last thing he wanted to do was go in here. But his foot needed attention, so he opened the door.

The Heroes' Haven was also called The Last Chance Saloon and never referred to by its real name, the speaking of which brought bad luck. The Terminal Ward. The perfume projector inside could not quite conceal the taint of living decomposition, the muted Muzak was penetrated by the gurgled groans of the dying, the soft monotone squeals of telltale machines announcing the deaths of their hook-ups during the evening. Bill looked wildly in all directions but there was no sign of Doctor Delazny!

"Bowb and damn!" Bill snarled, wheeling around to get the hell out of here. In mid-wheel, however, he spotted something that caught him up short, gave him pause.

It was a shelf of lozenge-books! And they looked *whole*! Unstripped! Bill was very bored, and he could use a whole book to read. The doomed at the hospital must get special privileges, he thought. Of course the irony was they'd never finish reading the books anyway.

He examined the titles. E-I-E-I-O! by Greg Bore. PLANET OF THE ALIEN TRANSVESTITE PANTY RAIDERS Vol. VI. THE WELL OF GENITALS by Jerk el Upchucker. NIGHT OF THE LIVING CHINGERS by Stephen Thing. Boy! *Classics!*

Still, he couldn't take more than one, so Bill selected a shining lozenge labeled BLEEDER'S DIGEST. This contained ten condensed books especially prepared for the consumption of people who didn't have very long to live.

Good enough! This should keep him going for awhile, thought Bill as a death rattle in a nearby throat spurred him on his away.

Of course, he'd *boil* the damned thing first this time. His nose twanged in response for his nose knew another nose nosed ahead by a nose.

But if Bill had been nosier he would have noticed the alien electronic eyeball at the end of its periscope, scrutinizing his activities and transmitting them to tiny reptilian eyeballs, deep below the hospital.

CHAPTER 3

THE HAZARDS
OF BEACHCOMBING

WHAT A WONDERFULLY MEDIOCRE DAY TO be half-alive, thought Bill.

Tiny waves surged idly up the dun-colored beach. A greenish-orange sun sat over the horizon like a bloated and festering fruit. A bank of leaden clouds was slowly drawing across the sky, thankfully shuttering out the sickly light with torn, damp gray veils. The smell of rotting fish assaulted Bill's already tortured nose as he walked along the deathly still sea. He sneezed hugely and wiped his nostrils with the back of his hand. His morale slumped to rock bottom and remained heavily there.

Ah, yes! What a wonderful place for R and R, thought Bill. Permission had been reluctantly granted to him to go out for a morning stroll. Get some fresh air. Ha!

What a bowby joke! He half-wished they'd shipped him to Dental School World. At least they had nitrous oxide dispensers on every corner there, guaranteeing a lift and quick high whenever you needed it. Which, of course, was all the time.

Still, a Trooper took what he could get, cursing and complaining the entire time. The bar was still closed, all of his own booze long drunk and he couldn't find Dr. Delazny. In desperation he figured maybe a little exercise might do him good before he settled down with a newly steamed-and-cooled BLEEDER'S DIGEST.

Bill had taken off his shoes to walk on the beach. He turned back and contemplated the tracks he'd left in the sand, being sluggishly lapped at by the now snotgreen sea. A regular human foot, along with a good-sized cloven hoof! Wouldn't an exploring xeno-biologist get a wrinkled brow and excited jollies over that!

Perhaps a little wade would cool his tootsies. He took a flat rock and skipped it over the surface of the water. A fish hurtled up out of the sea, roaring angrily, caught it in a great gaping mouth, and flopped back into the water, leaving the flash of sharp gleaming fangs on Bill's retina.

Bill stopped. Oh well. He didn't really feel like swimming anyway. He was a simple man, with simple needs and even simpler pleasures. All of them involving the opposite sex. Or food. Or drink. Or dope. Or, preferably all of them at the same time. Or best of all out of the Troopers—but that would never be. Unfortunately, walking along the beach barefoot, contemplating this good ole quixotic Motherbowber Nature, did not involve any of these. He sighed mightily, sneezed explosively, then went back to get his shoes, and head back for the hospital, where surely the bar would be open and he could make his simpler pleasures even simpler.

Walking back, he got a good view of the water—and the dehydrator plant past the hospital, belching forth great black greasy gobs of smoke. What was in this seawater anyway? Bill wondered absently. Some godawful gunge, no doubt. He went up a little closer to inspect the dark stuff.

It looked a little like treacly black beer, or the infamous Von Guinness Stout from the green sun-bathed shores of Paddy's Planet, thought Bill. There was even a tan foam that flecked the wavelets. This made Bill even thirstier for some good brew. Not that the hospital served anything near as good as Von Guinness. Bill strongly suspected that the stuff on tap was closer to the blendered contents of the cloacus magnus spiked with formaldehyde. But it got him drunk enough, and his accepted practice was never to question an alcoholic drink too strongly.

He was just about to pull back from the edge of the sea, when about five yards out, a foamy eruption of water geysered up. The spray splattered back down, but the subject that had caused it remained, dark and dripping.

"Hi, big feller!"

For several moments, elation filled Bill. Standing in the water was a naked woman, her high-nippled breasts rising triumphantly and expansively in the air, her oval and beautiful face animated by an expression of rampant sensuousness.

By the Sacred Spirit of great Ahura Mazda, thought Bill hopefully. I'm going to be sexually attacked!

She began to walk toward him, rising up out of the foam—and the few precious moments of elation ended. From the waist down, the woman's flanks were covered by thick, goatish hair, the same dark brown as the mane of long wet stuff dripping down her aquiline features.

When she walked up to the beach, Bill saw that the legs narrowed to two cloven hooves very much like his own, but much more petite.

"Hello," said Bill. "Glad to make your acquaintance, if even so briefly but, well, I gotta be going. I have an appointment to get a shot for a real virulent case of an unspeakable disease that I dare not speak about!" He stumbled backward, but his foot (the moody one, natch) chose a particularly soft batch of sand to step upon, and he lost his balance and fell.

The goat-lady continued walking toward Bill undeterred, licking her lips in a most lascivious manner. This close she looked like a walking gynecological close-up from GALACTIC HUSTLERHOUSE MAGAZINE.

"You're kind of ugly," she husked in a husky voice. "But you've got an okay bod—and just one *heck* of a nice foot!"

Bill howled with horror and tried to get up and run away. With amazingly strong hands, the strange woman grabbed Bill's belt and hauled him back.

"Really, ma'am—it's not my foot! I mean, if you really like it, *take* it!" Bill was only sorry that it was so firmly attached. Perhaps if it hadn't been, though, it would have been long gone by now.

"Ah, c'mon, Trooper. Don't you want to play footsie with me?"

Bill didn't. He just wanted to get away. Unfortunately, for all his hard-packed, well-trained muscle, the pretty but frightening goat-lady held him, unmoving in her grip. She seemed to have incredible power stashed somewhere in those slender arms, that well-proportioned back. She hauled Bill back to the sea, leaving behind two deep furrows where his scrabbling hands tried to find purchase in the sand.

"Noooooooooooo!" said Bill. The "No" turned into wild screaming as the lukewarm, foul water folded over his legs.

"Take a deep breath, big guy. I can tell you're already in over your head about *me!*"

So saying, and cackling hoarsely with insane alien glee, the female satyr dragged the thrashing and splashing and yowling Bill down into the mysterious, murky sea.

CHAPTER 4

THE MYTHING LINK

GLUG, THOUGHT BILL.

Glugity, bowby glug.

He seemed to be drifting now in a deep dark bowl of licorice-flavored gelatin, the kind that Eager Beager used to scarf up so happily at Camp Leon Trotsky. Bill had always given that military nutcase his portion of dessert, as did many of the recruits. Not out of generosity—that wasn't the Troopers' way!—but only because it was completely inedible. Eager Beager didn't actually eat them all, only some. Most he used for boot polish.

Down, down into the licorice gelatin went Bill.

Glug, gurgle, and glack.

His life flashed before his eyes.

Since it hadn't been much of a life, though, he had to

go into repeats, and then syndication.

Finally, though, when the black stuff got immensely black and thick, and it looked like Bill was about to cash in his credits, he suddenly found himself floundering and squishing on dry land, spouting out water like a beached whale.

Then, just as oxygen restored his heartily heaving lungs to full capacity, somebody turned out the lights, and he plunged yet again into total darkness.

"Rosebud!" was Bill's last thought as he began to drown.

Consciousness focused slowly, like a gently erotic cinematic fade-in.

Bill awoke to birdsong. Sweet zephyrs danced over his hair, and he heard the tinkle of laughter, the gentle swirl of a gently plonking musical instrument. All these things were very nice, and Bill felt relaxed and calm. He could have just lain there for languid hours, but for the sweet acrid smell that suddenly wafted to his nostrils.

Boing! went his eyelids as they sprang wide open.

Wine!

In Bill's top ten list of favorite libations containing CO_2HO_2O, wine was maybe number nine, with Sterno as number ten and good old brain-destroying grain alcohol with all its varied applications leading the pack. But then, when did a Trooper get to dally with fancy stuff like el vino? Bill had gotten drunk on dingleberry wine on Squat IV once in a particularly rancid cantina on leave from Latrine Attendant Qualifying Training, and the hangover the next day was a memory that still disturbed him when he was distressed. But this stuff he was smelling smelled real good, and hey! Alcohol was alcohol and the only time that Bill was uninterested in alcohol was when he had to drive a starship. (Footnote: Free Public Service Announcement from Galactic Troopers Against Drunk Driving.) But then, since Bill wasn't a starship pilot, had no intention of being one, and was frightened bowbless at the thought, he very seldom had to worry.

His eyes rolled about. His stomach clutch engaged, then ground into gear. Saliva gushed into his mouth, drooling down and dripping off one of Deathwish Drang's fangs.

"Hi there, you-all!" he croaked. "Anybody got something to *drink* here?"

The sight that met his eyes, however, stopped all thoughts of gross guzzling.

He lay sprawled in an olive grove, lightly kissed by gentle lightbeams radiating warmly from a stylized sun in the heavens. This same sky was bluer than a robin's egg in deep depression. In the distance mighty mountains reached skyward, while, just yards away, he discerned the tell-tale flora of a vineyard. He was lying on luxurious soft grass, even more cushiony than the Port-a-lawns in the Officer's deck on Imperial battle cruisers. Flowers speckled the green with vibrant colors worthy of an Impressionist painter's most blobbily intense splatters.

But it was not the overwhelming beauty of the scenery that surprised Bill most, but rather the festivities, the caprices capering about him. Scantily clad women giggled as they darted amongst the bushes. Horned furry satyrs frenetically pursued these young women—or lounged about, being fed grapes from glistening purple bunches. Philosophical types in toga-like folds of white cloth, wearing laurel leaves upon their aged brows, spouted metaphysical theory—while ogling young boys from the corner of their eyes—pausing in their orations only to grab the occasional passing ephebe buttock.

And *all* of these merry-makers held huge jeweled goblets aswim with fragrant purple liquid, constantly being topped off by leafy dryads carrying pitchers of wine.

By the eternal benevolence of Ahura Mazda in all his magnificence, though Bill really hadn't been to church lately, this was something! What an incredible *party!*

"What a brave new world, that hast such creatures in it!" came a voice, sweet as Bill's favorite childhood cereal, CORNDOG CRUNCHIES, with an entire dog in every stick.

"Huh?" he sussurated vibrantly. The words had come from behind him, and Bill swiveled his head.

"Oh sweet prince!" the voice sounded again, as vibrant as a silver bell. "Never have I looked upon a visage so lovely. May I dare request humble permission to kiss an ivory fang!"

Bill found himself staring into a set of the most beautiful blue eyes he had ever seen. These were sticking out of a face that would have launched a thousand starships! As well as a body that would have launched a thousand starship Troopers! All of this fascinating femaleness clothed in the barest minimum of silken gowns, the maximum of blonde hair and honey-soft skin!

What a *package of palpitating pulchritude!*

He was about to hurl himself upon her, wrap her in the generosity of his embrace, rain kisses on those fulsome lips, and all the other bowb he read about in the romance magazines, when he was brought up short, suddenly remembering the circumstances from which he'd just arrived.

"Where am I?" he said, with great and boring lack of imagination and/or intelligent response, sitting up. He was still clothed in his hospital jumpsuit, still in his bare feet, and one of those feet was still hairy, and, it must be mentioned, also sported a cloven foot. In his hand he still clutched the BLEEDER'S DIGEST lozenge. Absently, he slipped this into a pocket, and eyed his surroundings with beady and suspicious eyes.

"Why, don't you know, darling?" said the fair young woman. "You are in the fabled Fields of Ozymandias. Not very far from the even more highly valued Fields of Elysium! Pray tell, good sir, what sort of fabulous mythic creature are *you*?"

He looked back at the beautiful woman, and was immediately hypnotized and paralyzed by the radiant complexion, the pearly teeth, the immense breasts scarcely covered by the chintziest wisp of gauze. "I'm an Imperial Trooper Drill Instructor, Unskilled, Horny."

"Hmm! Never heard of those, but then you must be from the Halls of Hades to possess such a visage of delight! You are, dare I say it, *awfully* handsome. Can I get you some wine, a large beaker let us say!"

Does the Emperor sit on the throne?

A very dazzled frazzled Bill could say nothing but "Uh—yeah!" and then watch as her plentifully portioned posterior wiggled wondrously away to get a goblet.

Bill realized that his heart was palpitating in a curious manner. Now, palpitations were no stranger to our intrepid Trooper whenever sighting desirable female flesh. Particularly palpitations of certain regions. But these stirrings were far more subtle, filled as they were with sighs and little tremblings in his abdomen.

Bill belched, and the abdomen problem stopped, but a kind of fuzziness strapped itself securely upon his brain.

Bill was in love, of the First Sight variety.

Naturally he wanted to consummate this passion immediately, and so waited impatiently for his belusted to return.

Instead, however, the female satyr popped her head around the bole of an olive tree and grinned lecherously at him.

"Yoo hoo! Big guy! You're awake!"

"You!" said Bill, disgust oozing from his lips and trickling down his chin. He got up and dusted himself off. He pointed a thick Trooper finger at his abductor. "Where the hell is this? Where the bowb did you take me to? Don't you know it's *treason* or worse to kidnap a Trooper of His Majesty's Imperial Forces?"

The female satyr bounced up provocatively and licked his finger with a horse-sized tongue. "But Sailor, I brought you here for purely heterosexual reasons. What are you, some kind of poof?"

Accusations of effeminacy are as bright red flags to virile Troopers like Bill, but the truth was at the moment Bill would far rather prove his sexual preference with the lady getting his wine. He had just enough bearing on the matter however, to again demand an answer. "This sure as hell doesn't look like Colostomy IV!"

"Oh! You mean the dreary planet I grabbed you from. Well, let's just say it is. . . . and it isn't. Now, tell me, which sexual position do you prefer?"

"With you? None!"

"What's wrong with you, guy? Most Troopers I grab are plenty hot to trot! You didn't get something shot off in the war or anything like that?"

At that moment, the voluptuous maiden of his dreams strolled back carrying a beaker of wine so large she had to use both hands.

"Zeus's caboose!" The satyr sighed. "The penny is finally dropping. I see that Irma got to you first!" The creature shrugged resignedly.

Irma raised lovely eyebrows as she swept her eyes over the Satyr. "Darling," she breathed icily, "You are about the ugliest poxy doxy I have *ever* seen. Anyway, I thought satyrs were all males!"

"We are, babe!" said the satyr, pulling off its wig and its strap–on breast prostheses. "But me, I like a little break now and then. See how the other half live." He pulled a cigar out of the bra–humidor and stuck it in his mouth and stomped off, giving the maiden a parting scowl.

This was far too much for Bill to take, sober. He grabbed up the wine that Irma held and downed several enormously hearty gluggs. He emerged gasping with pleasure, for this was the best wine he'd ever tasted, though of course he'd never actually had *true* wine before, anyway not the kind from stomped grapes.

Feeling much better, Bill looked at Irma, and his heart grew soft again. "Irma! What a nice name! I'm Bill."

"Thank you, Bill!"

"What's a nice girl like you doing in a place like this?"

"Why, I've been here a very long time! This is my home. I live anon in the Parthenon!"

"Anonymously?"

"Pardon?"

"Never mind." Bill took another few quick swallows to clear his head. "I still don't get it, though. I guess I've heard of myths and stuff from books and comics. But myths are supposed to be *myths*. I mean, if they were *real*, they wouldn't be myths, would they?"

Irma looked downcast. "You've found me out, Bill. You're quite right. I am not from this land. Like you, was untimely ripped from the womb of my gentle home planet."

She sat down against a bole of a tree and wept.

Bill drank some more wine and thought about this. When he looked at the maiden, his heart still went pitter-pat. A Trooper being a Trooper, he still wanted some fast and heavy action, but the iota of farm clodhopper still remaining in the core of his being was moved by this delicate flower of a woman.

"There, there," he said, thinking of words to comfort her. "Maybe some way-out, enthusiastic sex would make you feel better!"

"Oh, you male chauvinist pigs are all alike!" said Irma, and she wept yet more.

Now, Bill thought this was a compliment, and was touched deeply. "Look, I'll get us both out of here, Irma. But first we have to compare notes." In protracted and boring detail he outlined his origins, and how he'd been dragged here by the licentious satyr. Irma, blinking back perfect tears, sniffled and listened. Bill had to wake her up twice during the repetitious parts, but at least she *tried* to pay attention.

"Now it's your turn, Irma. Tell me your story."

So Irma did just that.

IRMA'S TALE
or
"Snow Job"

My full name is Irma Feritayl, and I'm from a planet called Fey in the Softscience system in the Half-Baked Sector of the Galaxy.

When I was a little girl, I had lots of kittens. Pretty little balls of fur, oh! such soft and cuddly creatures. I loved cats and kittens so much that the servants called me Kitten, and that's still my nickname if you want to call me that. Anyway, I had a kitten called Moonbeam and a kitten called Dusty and a kitten called Snowflake. They were such funny things, and they loved to play with yarn and scamper about. Oh, we had such fun! Did I tell you about my kitten called Mr. Furball? He had these strange gray spots all over his rear end. Anyway, these kittens when they became cats weren't psychic or anything, but I wish they had been, just like in the Snortin' Andy books I used to read. You know about those, don't you? Like GALACTIC PETS. And my favorite, BITCH WORLD. No? Oh, they're sooooo good... All the heroes and heroines are psychic and they can talk to animals! Oh, and did I tell you about the kitten I had called Sir Troublemaker. Well, when he became a cat...

Bill interrupted at this point and suggested that Irma get past the bit about the kittens and get to the point. *Any* point that wouldn't send him screaming out of his mind like this dreadful cat crap.

Oh, sure. So, did I mention I was a Princess? Yes, my father was King Hans Pagan Feritayl. What a wonderful father! He was the one who gave me all the kittens. And we had a family counselor named

Merfud. It was Merfud who divined that I was a Special! I don't know if you know what Specials are, but some people call them Talents and some call them Espers, and some planets just call them Nerds. Anyway, Merfud figured that my Specialness was that I could psychically speak to Unicorns! Unfortunately, as there were no Unicorns on Fey, I didn't get to use my specialness very much. But still I *knew* I was not only a Special, but a Special Princess!

But now the story gets sad. I was kidnapped by the evil Queen Snowjob in the country of Great Big Frosty Mountains when I was just a teenager. Worse, she spread a genetic curse on my father's land of Juvenile. Communicable Zits! Whew, was I glad I wasn't there! Did I tell you I had a boyfriend? Well, I did. His name was Joe. Joe and I both liked cats, which is why we got along so well. And also, Joe was a Special, too. Joe could talk to slugs. Unfortunately, that didn't help him much in his quest to rescue me. He didn't make it too far, either, before he died of Terminal Acne. Or that's what the evil Queen Snowjob told me, anyway. I found out pretty soon what Snowjob wanted from me. She wanted to rule the whole planet of Fey, change the orbit around the sun, and turn it into a galactic ski resort. She'd made a deal with the Chingers to get a Special Cosmic Unicorn shipped in to Fey—and she needed *me* to communicate with it!

Well, when I found out about this, I knew that I could *never* be a party to this evil plot. Daddy *hated* tourists! So I had to find a way out. And I did just that! I explored the lower regions of caverns and found a sewer grate. I opened it and with a lantern I navigated my way down deep into the sewer system.

I had been wandering a very long time, when I saw a light ahead! It was an opening! So I walked out . . .

And I found myself here.

When I looked around, though, the hole had closed up.

And so, here I've been stuck for what seems like forever.

The End

The beautiful princess called Irma sighed and put her head into her hands.

Bill rubbed her back sympathetically. Such a sad story. It was also the most incredible load of lachrymose bowb that he had ever heard. Only he didn't dare tell her that since he still had plans to get into her knickers. "You know, maybe a little sex would cheer you up!" he said brightly.

"Oh, Bill. Let us just forget awhile the crude lusts of the flesh! I think you are one of the most majestic creatures I have ever seen. May we simply commune from soul to soul?"

"Soul to soul? Isn't that a Galactic Motown record by Outta Sight and the Pimps?" Bill said.

"No, silly! It's a form of Romantic Psychic Telepathy, just like in BLAZING ROMANTIC SCIENCE COMIX!"

And when she flashed her baby blues at him, Bill simply turned to silly putty in her hands. Having drunk the entire goblet of wine may have had something to do with this malleable state, but actually Bill was in fact as smitten as his tough Trooper training would allow.

And so, for a time, the sweet object of his affection communed with Bill's soul on a spiritual plane, which did absolutely but nothing for him. And it really had been a long day. Clutching her warm hand in his he drowsed off and communed with some heavy zzzzzzzz's.

CHAPTER 5

THE RAPE OF IRMA

LIGHTNING, ACROSS A BLOODSHOT LAND-scape.

Thunder, banging out like a brobdingnagian belch accompanied by the wail of a thousand petulant pussies.

Bill woke up—vaguely—to spaghetti.

Color-coded spaghetti, wound into a coil, snaking away into machines, chugging and clicking, needles needling, dials dialing.

A squeaky voice: "Partial consciousness, Unit Alpha V!"

Another voice, chalk on a blackboard: "Dampen! Dampen!"

"Endorphins at optimum level already. Unit resisting

unconsciousness. Awareness level reaching drugged but dangerous level."

Bill groaned. Where the hell was he? He saw stretches of stainless steel stained by little green amorphous blobs.

Focus! He had to focus. Where the hell was his Trooper discipline?

"Well then, slug him again, you idiot!"

A mass of resonant density fell directly upon Bill's noggin, and once more this particular Starship Trooper saw the stars.

When Bill awoke the next time again, he found his head in the sweetly scented lap of his beloved Irma. She was stroking his hair and gently rambling on about the delights of pussies.

". . . and then there was Featherhead! Oh, that cat just *adored* his catnip! Of course, we had to get him de-clawed after he scratched that poor serf's eyes out, but oh well!"

Bill scrunched around and was rewarded with a mag-nificent upshot view of Irma's magnificently impressive breasts expanding above him, blocking out the view completely. Which was all right with him.

What a Heaven!

What Paradise!

What an incredible existence! Who cared where the hell he was! Bill immediately decided that wherever he was it was lightyears better than anywhere the Troopers could send him.

With satiated pleasure the lovebirds talked and sipped the clear wine for a brief eternity beneath an Aegean sun, not too far at all from the wine-dark sea, and just down the hill from Mt. Olympus, while sprites and songsters, dancers and satyrs played with Maypoles and whiled away the day with more of this kind of bucolic, fresh air Bacchanalian stuff.

Bill could not remember when he had been happier. Though to be precise Bill could not remember ever being happy, but it does not pay to split hairs: for a gentle two or three hours the sun shone, orgone surged through Bill's body and his sperm-filled eyeballs swelled mightily under the pressure. He was relaxed and content, caught up in the fanciful spell woven by the climate, the wine, and the concupiscent creature prattling incontinently on beside him.

Little did this happy-for-an-instant Trooper realize that this happiness would be oh, so brief.

Irma had suggested a walk.

She was an enchanting creature, the stuff of pure dreams. Bill had never encountered a woman like her before. To Bill, women were not mysterious beings; mystery implies intellectual thought, and all Bill's thoughts on the subject were unambiguously coitus connected. Except for his mother, of course. Bill's memories of her were pretty vague and he was sure that she had been kind and gentle; but he couldn't really remember. Which meant that memories of an earlier, possibly gentler existence had been entirely driven out by sadistic Trooper training and his loathsome experiences in the wars. Still, Bill had a soft spot in his heart for Mom; somehow he'd eluded the usual Trooper heart surgery on the subject.

Yes, he feebly remembered the days with Mom back on Phigerinadon II. He remembered the lullabies she used to sing, "Song of the Passionate Porkuswine" and "Ole Girl River" in her slightly grating, off-key soprano. Bill remembered the chocolate-soy brownies she would nuke in their homey homemade atomic-wave oven that had accidentally killed Dad. He remembered her gentle whippings with the robo-mule prod when she caught him reading WANKY TRI-D COMICS on the Sabbath instead of studying the Neo-Koranic Texts According to the Subgenius Bowb of the Zoroastrian Nabobs for his religious upbringing. He remembered how she had smelled of sour groundhog yogurt, and the way their kitty-kebab suppers tended to stick on her mustache and nostril hairs. He remembered the wonderful soft blue of her skin when she would have those circulatory problems she was wont to. (Poor Mom! Parts were always falling off her at the most inopportune moments.)

But most of all, he remembered how Mom would rock him to sleep as a child when he had the colic. She'd put on some old blitz c-nodes and make Bill dance to near-exhaustion, urging him on with blasts from their old microwave gun warming the seat of his pants. When she finally allowed his little head to hit the pillow, Bill tended to fall asleep immediately.

Yes, dear Mom was a creature apart from all other women, and Bill treasured those trace elements he had left of her in the burnt-out neural banks of his shriveled gray matter.

Other women?

Well, there were the licensed hookers of course. Bill seldom attained a higher level than the two bucks for two minutes variety to whom he was joyfully addicted. Occasionally he had glanced with lurking lust at the hard-bitten Trooper females. But since they tended to wear aluminum bras and chain mail panties, keeping their skulls shaved for easy node-implants, Bill hardly thought of them as sexual objects. (Far too many Troopers tended to get their joy-plugs burnt if they tried the fleshy interface with one of them.) And then of course there had been Meta. But even Meta, with all her wildly exuberant female attributes, her high octane sexuality and her 90 proof pheromones, was hardly what you would classify as classically feminine.

Irma was.

In fact, she was not only classically feminine; she was feminine *classically*. She was sweet and gentle, her words kittenishly playful and teasing at times. But she could also listen, jaw agape, to what Bill had to say. With those big, round blue eyes full of awe; eyes that Bill could fall into, could drown in their great blue lake of wonder. He coughed and spat lachrymosely, intoxicated not merely with the huge amount of wine he'd downed, but by the subtle shifting of her scent, of her lithe limbs beneath the gauzy gown; the way her gentle fingertips would occasionally touch his swelling biceps to emphasize a point.

Little did Bill realize it, but here he encountered a threat far worse to his well-being as a Trooper than any Death-Juggernaut of the Ether, any Fry Ray of the Cosmos that the dreaded Chingers could throw at him.

Bill was falling in *love*.

They held hands.

They baby-talked to one another. (As this was a step up in Bill's language skills, he couldn't do it very long.)

They told each other their deepest longings. (Irma wanted a new kitty-cat, and Bill wanted a bottle of Old Granbowb.)

They walked in springtime freshness while lovebirds chirped amidst the olive branches and doves cooed softly and musically at their feet, occasionally squawking as they were stepped on.

Since the doves looked terribly delicious, Bill would have blasted one for dinner, if he'd had a blaster on his belt. Instead, he made a grab for one, caught it around the neck and would have wrung that neck, but for Irma's horrified remonstrations.

"But I'm hungry!" said Bill with no little amount of frustration. "What do you guys eat here!"

"Why, ambrosia, of course!"

Bill looked down at the thrashing dove, and then looked suspiciously at Irma. Memories of the terrible reconstituted food on that grand old lady of the space fleet, the CHRISTINE KEELER, bubbled loathsomely in Bill's memory. Here was fresh meat in his hand, as opposed to questionable victuals from Irma.

"It's *very* good!" said Irma.

"Hey, is that a rainbow over there?" said Bill, pointing.

"Where?" Irma spun around and searched.

With deft flicks of his wrists, Bill stuffed the dove down the front of his jumpsuit. Just in case ambrosia was anything akin to starship galley chow.

"I don't see any rainbow," said Irma, turning and looking at him, batting her pretty eyelashes with bemusement. "Where's the dove?"

"Oh, he flew away." Bill grabbed her hand. "But, dearest creature, let us not dwell on dreary doves but speak of other more tender things. Let's walk away further down there, all right?"

"Down there" was a nice private little dip in the field, a gully where some gentle brook doubtlessly burbled merrily. Bill's intentions were, of course, entirely unchivalrous. They'd drink the jug of wine that dangled from the goat-skin that Irma had scrounged somewhere and he wouldn't hog it at all but would let Irma get just a wee bit tipsy. Then he'd suggest an innocent skinny-dip in the sparkling water. And then, when she got ahold of his manly physique and her feminine juices started mixing it up with the alcohol—whamo!—she'd be putty in his hands. What a way to go! What a snazzy plan!

However, no sooner had they reached the edge of this delightful scene, (and there was indeed a most delightful burbling brook here, Bill saw with great interest) than a sudden sharp screeching tore through the enchantment, like a schoolteacher's claws on the 3-D board!

"Screeeeeeeeeeeeeeeeech!" went the ghastly sound, somehow contriving to fill the entire universe with its gigantic gurgling. Somewhere buried in that terrible sound was pulsing music as well.

"What the bowb is that?" said Bill.

"Oh dear," said Irma, looking up resignedly. "We have ventured too far out into the open. I forgot that

Zeus desires to slake his lusts upon my maiden loins."

Zeus sure wasn't the only one, Bill thought, but what did that have to do with that noisome *noise*?

He looked up, and was immediately stricken by quivering, shaking, quaking fear. Descending quickly from the sky, its black form obscuring the sun, was a monstrous bird shedding mites the size of grapefruit. Wrapped around its neck were gigantic speakers. The result was a frightening avian ghetto blaster mutation!

And was that the Phigerinadon II national anthem it was playing? "In Awe We Kiss the Emperor's Big Toe. Pyakh." No it wasn't. It was an archaeological treasure from the dawn of time sung by Elvis Pelvis.

"Omigod!" cried Bill. "What is it?"

"It's a Rocker!" cried Irma. "Oh, please, Bill—don't let it *get* me! Be my *hero*!"

Bill's mighty sinews bunched, preparing for battle. His awesome fangs bared, his fists fisted, he took his stance against the creature, and looked up to snarl out his challenge.

He saw the flash of scythelike talons, the gnash of the sharp, giant beak, the glint of murder in its huge black eyes—

Bill immediately turned and ran for his life.

"Bill!" cried Irma despairingly. "Bill, don't *leave* me!"

Bill kept on running. He glanced backward as he ran to see if the Rocker was following. Fortunately for him, it wasn't. Instead it was descending upon the hapless Irma, wings furling down and flapping up a horrendous wind that struck Bill in the face like a slap. He watched as the creature hovered above Irma and curved its talons around her.

The gauzy robe ripped and fluttered as the creature seized her. With a squawk and the audial sneer of Elvis, the Rocker took flight again, soaring high and flapping toward the distant mountains, gusting up a great cloud of dust.

Bill stood and gaped, coughing in the dust.

The fear gradually seeped away and deep regret took its place.

A solitary lonely tear dripped down his cheek, across his lip and onto his fang—where it mixed with saliva and slopped down onto his cloven hoof.

What a terrible loss!

Thoughts of incipient sex sprouted wings and flapped away in the trail of the Rocker.

"Hey!" called a voice behind him.

Bill spun around. Standing there with a thoughtful look was the formerly female satyr.

"By the way, the name is Bruce," said the satyr, extending a hand. Still stunned, Bill shook the hand.

"What. . . . What was *that?*"

"Hey, we mythological creatures have got our problems! It ain't all nectar and ambrosia and hot juicy lust here, ya know? All kinds of loathsome monsters would just as soon eat you as look at you. Why, just last week the Labor Union finally got ahold of poor old Hercules and made him cough up dues." The satyr named Bruce quavered in fear and emitted a pungent goat-smell. "Anyway, that there's Zeus' Rocker. Old Zeus is the king of the Gods, and he's been hankering after a taste of Irma's flank steaks. Jumped her once as a swan, but Irma got him by the neck and near throttled him. Looks like you guys just walked too far out into the open."

"Where did he take her?" Bill asked, realizing with a sinking heart that no other woman would be able to satisfy his unrequited desires like Irma could.

"Oh! Up yonder, onto the top of Mt. Olympus. That's where the Palace of the Gods is!" Bruce noticed the lump in Bill's jumpsuit. "Hey, pal. Is that your lute, or are you just happy to see me?"

"Huh? Oh, it's a dove I found a little while ago. Kept it in case I needed a little snack."

Bill took the dove out and was not pleased to see that

it had suffocated during its incarceration. He looked unhappily at its limp, dead corpse, feathers fluttering down to the ground.

Bruce gasped and staggered back. "Gurgle!" he gurgled. "You didn't. . . ."

"Didn't what . . . ?"

"You are really in the merda now, bub!" His little eyes bugged out like Greek olives amidst his wilting saladlike hair. "That there's one of the Doves Above! You kill one of those and. . . ."

A trembling whir of wind. A harsh rattle of thunder.

"And here they *come*! Not only that—I just happened to remember that they still want me for putting the blocks to their changeling!"

"Who?" asked Bill.

"The Furries, man. The Furry Eumensuckadees!"

With no further adieu, the beast man started to run gallop toward the olive groves. But he'd gotten no further than ten yards away when a dazzling sizzle of lightning split the air like the crack of Doom. A bright bolt seared down, striking the satyr directly in the keester, frying him on the spot. When the smoke cleared, all that was left was a rotary spit of roasted gyro meat.

Stunned, Bill turned around to see who had hurled this incredible bolt of fire, and was immediately confronted by the third most astonishing thing he had ever seen. (What numbers two and one are will be revealed later on.)

Riding an island of moiling, electricity-shot clouds, were three stern-looking lasses in Bill Blass business suits, carrying briefcases in one hand, and copies of INTERSTELLAR MS. and GALACTIC SAVVY in the other.

"You!" bellowed one, and a stream of lightning shot down, hurtling between his legs and blasting the ground not a yard from Bill's butt. "Move further and kiss the family jewels goodbye!"

This sounded anatomically improbable, but Bill none-theless decided it would be best to heed the command, since the smell of charred lamb and garlic in the air was a heavy reminder of Bruce's fate. "I'm convinced!" he shrieked. "I'm not moving! Don't zap me!"

The ladies murmured amongst themselves, then one leaned down off the cloud, scrutinizing Bill, distaste edging suspicious anger. "My name is Hymenestra, leader of the Furries. Guardians of the Doves Above! Our mystical needles have hopped off their moorings! We have reason to believe that one of our sacred charges hast been stricken down, yea, unto Death! Knowest thou ought of this, mortal?"

Bill grimaced, trying to keep the dead dove hidden behind his back. "No, gee. Absolutely nothing!"

One of the other ladies leaned over the edge of the clouds, peering down upon the ground. "My name is Vulvania. Whyest do I seest *bird* feathers strewnest about yon area?"

"Uhm," said Bill. "Bruce and I, er, uhm . . . We were having a pillow fight. Yeah! That's what was happen-ing!"

The third lady leaned over and pointed a stiff finger. "My name is G-spotstra. Whatest is that you are ob-scuring behindest thy posterior, mortal?"

"Hmm? Oh, this? What's that doing here?" Bill took out the dove. Its wings and head hung down patheti-cally; somehow the letter X had appeared over both of its eyes. "Oh! Yes, Bruce . . . Remember? The satyr you cooked over there. Yes. He asked me to hold on to it. Old Bruce smells pretty good. You ladies wouldn't have some pita bread and some lemon on you, would you?"

The ground seemed to shake with thunder as Hy-menestra roared. "Lying male abomination! Of cour-sest, that isest the general description of thy breed! Thou hastest killed one of our Doves! Oh woest uponest thou head!"

More thunder crashed, more lightning flashed. The

ladies conferred amongst one another, muttering vile imprecations. Bill decided that the heat of a pulsar beam battle between Chinger dreadnoughts and Empire cruisers was a far preferable place to be.

"Very wellest!" cried Hymenestra after the lengthy conference. "We chargest thou with guilt, pure and simplest! Thou hast killed a sacred Dove! We perceive that you are a man of war! How like all men! So eager to perpetrate death and destruction upon thyest neighbor at the slightest provocation! Very well, you have brought our curse down upon you, insect! Be-est thou visited with the Grime of the Aging Marinator!"

The ladies suddenly heaved up great masses of glop from the bottom of their cloud and chucked these at Bill. His Trooper reflexes jerked his body away from the first splash of glop, but the second caught him full in the face, and he could feel the third striking him in the midsection. The stuff had the consistency of pureed roc guano and had the astringent stench of bilge water at the bottom of a sea-cruiser after a week-long rum party below-decks. Bill felt himself being hurled about willy-nilly by forces of which he had no conception.

When the shaking had ceased, he found himself face first staring at trampled grass, quite dirty and quite confused. He heaved himself up off the ground, and wiped the odorous stuff from his face and body. In doing so, his hands hit upon something that hung from his neck. Very quickly, he determined that it was the dead dove, its breast pierced by a leather thong, which in turn was tied around his neck.

Moreover, the dove was beginning to stink.

Bill, of course, made to take this off. However, the knot in the leather thongs seemed to have defied his mud-slippery fingers.

"Beholdest thou the Curse of the Grime of the Aging Marinator!" bellowed the voice of Hymenestra from On High. "Thou canst not remove the dead avian until thou satisfiest two conditions. Onest:

"Thou must rescue she whom ist the love of thy life and give voice to thy tendermost feelings.

"Twoest A: Thou must seek the answer to the age-old question: How canst personskind achieve peace in our time, obtain a truce withest the Chingers, and live happily ever after.

"Twoest B: (It's a corollary) Verily, whyest dost thou hairy monstrosities called 'men' rejoice in war, mindless lust, strong drink and Sunday afternoon anti-gravball."

"Gosh," snarled Bill. "Why don't you ask me the find the Meaning of Life as well."

"Oh, we women *know* that, silly," said one of the Furries slyly. "Now be-est off with you and heed the curse and solve our request, for sure as the dove that you have murdered rots, so rottest thy soul, and perhaps eventually the root-spot of thy short and curlies!"

With a thunderclap and a blast of fire, the Furries were suddenly gone, leaving behind only the smell of sulfur, brimstone and the toiletries section of Galactic Harrods-Bloomingdales.

Bill clutched his crotch reflexively at the very thought of the last threat. The thought of a groin transplant was enough to chill his very marrow. He'd had enough problems with his foot! Imagine if he got stuck with a mood pe—

"No!" he cried out, shutting out the very idea. "I'll get out of this. Somehow!"

First, the true love bit. Well, clearly in this case, the Furries meant Irma. He'd have to traipse after her and save her from Zeus, up there on Mount Olympus.

Fine. But then that other bit—peace with the Chingers? This sounded awfully suspicious, but what could he do? He didn't want to go around his entire life with a dead and moldering dove around his neck. It would make a big impression back in the barracks. His recruits would laugh him right off the drill field! He tried again to take the thing off, but could not.

First, though, he went down to the bubbling brook he'd hoped to take Irma skinny-dipping in, and washed off some of the Grime.

Then, he went over to the roasted spit of Bruce meat, cut off a few hunks for the trip, and set out for the celestial home of the Home of the Gods, and a *mano a mano* with Zeus himself.

All in all, thought Bill, he'd rather be back in boot camp.

CHAPTER 6

A STARSHIP NAMED "DESIRE"

BILL CLIMBED THE MOUNTAIN.

Since his home planet of Phigerinadon II was a very flat world, and he'd yet to be assigned for battle duty or so-called rest upon a mountainous world, Bill had absolutely nil experience with climbing mountains.

However, his Trooper training, to say nothing of his rock-hard Trooper ex-farmer muscles, now served him in good stead. His legs worked like rusty pistons as he climbed up the narrow crevices and steep goat trails of Mount Olympus. For fuel, he ate the pieces of Bruce the Transvestite Satyr he had taken along which, while certainly being a novel diet to say the least, sustained capric-satyric life. Actually, they were very tasty, though for Bill's taste the garlic could have been a bit less pronounced, and some Chingerra sauce would be nice. Halfway up though he reached a kind of plateau and the climbing got easier and even a little boring, so he stuck his copy of BLEEDER'S DIGEST up his nose so that he could read as he climbed.

He could feel the device slide around inside his sinuses as it attached its electronic appendages. There was a muffled whirring sound as it did its work and a shuddering *frisson* as it attached itself to his brain.

A "mind's eye" screen appeared in his frontal lobes which he could read wonderfully well, as it superimposed orange words over his field of vision.

First up was a short catalog of the Read-a-Book's contents.

He selected an appropriate condensed novel and dug into the craggy prose even as his hands found holds in the craggy mountainside.

CRITTERS OF MYST AND MEMORY
by
Michael Huge-Jackson

Call me Conrad Hilton.

No, strike that. Call me Gunga Din.

Naw, just go ahead and call me Gus.

When I'm a professional wrestler, they call me Grandiose Gus, the Eternal Victor or some other such swill. They say I saved Earth from the swarms of Harpy creatures from Greekus Planetus, but hell, I was drinking lots of ouzo that week and it's all a blackout to me, so what the hay! All I know is that I woke up in the Parthenon with a hot blaster in my hands and the landscape looking like catharsis time in a Sophoclean tragedy. Phew, dead mythological critters everywhere!

Then again, maybe I'm making all this up.

That's what myths are, you know. Made-up stories with heroes and gods and things. Some of my critics say that I just make up all these stories and whisper them into the ears of my lovers, who promptly spread them all around Earth. Others say they've seen me furtively sneaking from the Library of New Alexandria with stolen copies of the Secret Writings of Joseph Campbell tucked under my trench coat.

Stuff and nonsense, of course. Truth is, while I generally keep a paperback copy of Edith Hamilton tucked into my chinos' back pocket to while away the boring bits of adventures, my real name is Philip Chandler from the mysterious world of Camelot. This Earth business started a few years ago when I was a private dick in Old LA, and the following narrative means to set the record straight.

It was a sunny day in the City of Angels, and I was lubricating the bore of my .38 with oil and the back of my throat with some Jack Daniels, when the babe strolled into my office.

"My name is Frigga Athena," she sang, her mammoth gazongas hammocked in a steel bra that shone like a healthy Double Sun system. "Are you Philip Chandler, Private Third Eye from the Secret World of Camelot?"

"That's right, sweetheart," I snarled in my best Humphrey Bogart lisp. "Exiled here on Earth by Merlin himself after I trumped out in a Dimensional Bridge game."

She heaved those magnificent breasts at me like calling cards. "I'm in dreadful trouble, Mr. Chandler." She was batting a pair of baby blues at me from a moviestar face, and was already batting a thousand with my pulse.

"Trouble is my business, ma'am," I told her. " 'Specially trouble involving Beautiful Mythologically Proportioned Blondes. So what the scoop? Lost your unicorn? Husband cheating on you with that slut Aphrodite?"

I offered her a glass of whiskey and she knocked it back like her tonsils were on fire. She sat down and

I got a blast of Lotus Eaters Perfume like Bargain Night at Nero Wolfe's hothouse. "It's my husband, you see. Loki Agonistes. He's being blackmailed for running guns to semi-magical Third World Revolutionary countries."

Loki Agonistes! Buddha on Crutches! My eyes rolled like catseye marbles at the very name! I managed to get my eyes back in their orbits after some blind groping on my desk, and made appropriate gasping noises.

"Christ, lady. I still got a couple thousand years left in this old bod! I fool around with people after Loki Agonistes and my karma will be in Hades' sling, and this section of my life will be included in the Egyptian BOOK OF THE DEAD, in the Dumb Dicks section!" I got up to show her out. "Why don't you try this buddy of mine. Lives in Sausalito on a houseboat called the Screwed Straight, name of Travis Watts. He handles the Metaphysical Detection. Me, I stick to pure Mythological stuff."

The broad's hopeful smile flip-flopped into a frown that almost touched her toes. "But Mr. Chandler, I want you!" Suddenly, those arms were around me, and I had a face full of galvanized mammaries and a snootful of pheromones that would have steamed up the testosterone of an Ice Giant in mid-winter. She started to grind against me. I supplied the bumps.

By the time a half-hour passed and I came up for air from some serious couch Olympics, I was on the case.

Little did I realize that if this was a cosmic card game I was just entering, I'd just pulled the Trump of Jerkoffs to play with.

"It's like this," she said breathily, smoking a cigarette and blowing the smoke into my ear. "There are these Three Weird Sisters, you see—"

* * *

"Hullo!"

The voice sounded like it came from a great distance and had been amplified by a wonky klaxon-speaker.

Bill blinked. He came out of his book-induced fugue. He willed the words to disappear from his vision, and they did, but only after the second try. He realized that he had stopped climbing. He was standing on a level plateau with marble-columned temples in the near distance. In the forefront of this scene, on the stone *agora* —that is, Greek marketplace, or meeting place or assembly or, you know, something like that—stood a thirty-meter-high gleaming-silver starship with a needle nose and fins that looked as though it would have been more at home on top of a trophy for bad pulp fiction awards than here on Olympus. In big lustrous curlicued letters on its side was a name: DESIRE. The entire scene had an amazing luster and sheen to it, like a movie matte: in the background, a magnificent silver moon was rising up over acrylic-blue and white mountains. The creatures and citizens in the background looked like cartoons and tended to wear ruffles at their arms and throats. In short, not very Greek at all. And Zoroaster! In the skies, the stars looked like stylized twinkles on Christmas trees!

Bill was flabbergasted, stunned. Unbelievingly, he felt his flabber—and it really was gasted!

The whole panorama looked like an animated poster done by the Kelly Freebees school of Art at the L. Ron Hubris University, the boys who did the artwork for Trooper recruiting posters!

He drifted toward it, so dazzled by the bravura colors and airbrush work that he barely noticed the stink of the dead dove that hung about his neck.

Bill was approaching the starship cautiously when suddenly a pneumatic door opened in its belly, and a rope ladder unwound down to the marble floor. By the time he'd reached the base, a figure had exited the starship and was descending the rope with reckless ease. He was a tall, handsome man, wearing a rhinestone eyepatch, bright orange epaulets, tastefully decorated with shining tinsel, and long shiny black boots. A metallic-orange sash was tied around his slender midsection and from this dangled a holstered hand-blaster on one side, and a menacing cutlass on the other. This highly impressive, not to say ferociously gaudy, figure dropped down the last eight feet, tripping and falling with a clatter onto his butt. Bill caught a decided whiff of lavender and rum. The man looked up, bemused, at Bill with one startling blue eye. The other was startlingly rhinestone.

"Arrrrrrr," he said in a voice like Blackbeard's after Remedial English Lessons. "Hyperboreals, me fellow bucko! Does life remind you of the junk that floats onto the beach in Tokyo Bay?"

"No. I don't think that I ever heard of Tokyo Bay."

"Me neither. Hudson Bay, more like. Right by Nyark City on Earth. I did a quick read once on fabled Earth, historical home of all mankind, now riven by the blasts of atomic war. Where was I?"

"In the middle of Hudson Bay, I think."

"Of *course,* dear boy. How bright you are! Anyway, medical detritus, junkie needles, old Charlie Parker records. Never mind. Name's Rick. Rick the Supernal Hero." He held up his hand to shake, which Bill promptly did, introducing himself.

"Hullo, I'm Bill. Spelled with two L's. Was that you who hailed me a moment ago?"

"Certainly was. Saw you coming up over the horizon with that dead dove around your neck, knew at once that you must be a mariner in the ocean of Life like your obedient servant!" He looked on his shoulder. "Arrrrr! Now where's me own little bird! Archimedes!" He yelled back to the door in the side of the splendiferous starship. "Archimedes, come down and meet another bird-fancier."

"Awwwwwwwwwwwk!" squawked a voice from above. "Pieces of shayte! Pieces of shayte!"

"Watch it, Bill. Archy's had the trots lately," warned Rick. "He will eat prunes, prunes, no stopping him. Literally."

A brilliant blue and green parrot suddenly hurtled through the hatchway, screeching like a banshee on fire, letting fly at the same time with a cloacal catapult. There was a spattering on all sides. Bill did a quick Aztec two-step and nimbly skipped aside. But Rick (the Supernal Hero) was a little slow on the uptake, or bombed out on dope or something, and he caught a portion of the stuff on his forehead. He cursed mellifluously as he pulled out a spare scarf and wiped his forehead. Then he put the scarf on his shoulder and waved the parrot down. In a dazzling flutter of cobalt and emerald Archimedes landed, farted psittacinely, and promptly turned his head sideways, suspiciously eyeing Bill.

"Awwwkkkk! Bird killer! Awwk! Avicide!"

"I was hungry," Bill whined apologetically. "I didn't know that this beaky bastard was sacred. And, anyway, what's it to you, bowb-bird?"

Bill had had enough of avian trouble by this time and he jabbed out a threatening forefinger at the parrot—which squawked angrily and promptly bit it. "Yeow," Bill howled and sucked the throbbing digit.

"Archimedes—do be nice to our guest. You *know* I can clone you in a blink of a bird's eye and get meself a *better* parrot. With better cloacal control. So you had better be good."

"Awwwwwwk! Archimedes good boy! Awwwkk! Who loves ya, baby?"

"Can't clone his pleasing personality, though," said Rick, giving the big bird a kiss on the beak. "Say Bill, interesting foot you got there. What gives?"

Bill looked down at his cloven hoof and scowled at the sight. He didn't feel like waxing enthusiastic about the mood foot explanation, which did not bear thinking about. Much too bizarre and depressing. When in doubt, lie, as the old Trooper motto ran. "I'm a fighting fool of a Galactic Trooper. Ran into a radiation storm in the course of my highly classified duties. I can tell you only that the foot, shall we say, *mutated!*"

"Why, that *must* be painful!"

"I can't tell you. That information is also classified."

"Well we really are a bundle of secrets! And a Trooper to boot. Which fact I find highly relevant. I have just lost me first mate to a case of venereal scurvy. I told the fool to use the impervium condoms if he was going to vacation in the Backdooria system. A *little* uncomfortable, yes. But what are a few peter abrasions compared to the horrifying alternative. Think he listened to me? Got a bad case of the Fades and just wasted away." Rick eyed Bill's considerable musculature appraisingly. "Don't suppose you'd be interested in signing on as First Mate. Got meself a Quest coming up, and I could use a little qualified help."

"Sorry, pal. I've got to find a girl named Irma. She's my true love, and locating her is the only way I'm going to get this decaying dove off my neck." Racked now by self-pity, sniffing with sorrow, Bill explained the whole sad story, all the way from the hospital on Colostomy IV to the business with the Rocker and Zeus.

"Awwwww! Zeus! Zeus!" The parrot opened its eyes wide, squawked with fear, crapped copiously onto his master's shoulder, then flapped noisily back into the starship, screeching hideously as he flew.

"Does Zeus like parrot stew or something?"

"No, actually the oversexed deity got ahold of poor Archimedes after he swanned Leda, if you get my drift. Traumatized poor Arch. But it just so happens, completely by chance—but what else is serendipity for—that my Quest is taking me to one of Zeus's main hangouts."

Bill frowned. "You mean, he's not here on the pinnacle of Mount Olympus?"

Rick laughed. "Olympus shimpus! The summit of the mount is about ten thousand feet further up. This is just a Johnson Howard's Space Traveler's Comfort station." He pointed out the dark green building beyond a boulder that Bill had missed. "Had meself a hankering for about fourteen of the Three Hundred and Twenty-Eight Flavors."

"Could you give me a lift up to Olympus, Rick? This bird is really starting to rot." Bill's nose cringed as he looked down at the dead dove. Flies buzzed around the thing; the x's in the corpse's eyes x'ed back at him emptily.

"Yes, 'tis getting a little ripe, ain't it. Well, me hearty! I'll make you a deal. You come along with me, be my first mate, and I'll put that avain in a stasis field. Be my first mate and we'll probably find Zeus at his favorite watering hole—the destination of my Christian quest!"

"And what is that?" asked Bill suspiciously. Christians had a generally bad reputation on Phigerinadon II, ever since that Holy Roller show had held a revival on the Phalanges Continent amongst the Donner Settlement. The Hyper-Donners, being cannibals, had of course eaten these missionaries—and had suffered terrible bouts of indigestion for years afterwards. Hence the bad reputation.

"Why, for the second most fabulous quest of them all!" said Rick in a highly oratorical manner. "The Quest for the Holy Bar and Grill!"

Bill smiled enthusiastically. "Where do I make my mark!"

CHAPTER 7

FIRST MATE BILL

AFTER ALL THE MYTHOLOGICAL BOWB HE'D been traipsing through, it was nice to get onto a starship again. True, it wasn't precisely as comfortable as a Trooper starship, which made it the general galactic equivalent of a riveted steamboat without extras, but after the heavy G-force take-off almost mashed his face into a pulp, he learned his duties as first mate. For the most part these consisted of cleaning up the parrot droppings from the floors, walls, and even the ceiling—this parrot was really an aerobatic crapper—and dumping the results into the hydroponics room. What pleasure to realize that he had finally become a Technical Fertilizer Operator! Thus fulfilling his life-time ambition. It was an easy life, even if it was a crappy job, easier than the

Troopers, and Bill quickly got pretty used to things. Also, Rick was as good as his word on the dove business—he'd gotten out a can of "Loo Stasis," a special electronic fix for noisome starship heads, and gave the bird a good blast. The smell had ceased immediately, and would theoretically stay away for a couple of months. Of course he still couldn't get it off his neck, and if you touched the thing with a finger you'd get zapped by static electricity, but it was a small price to pay for containment of bird-rot stench.

Once this problem was solved, and Bill had learned his other responsibilities as first mate, the days settled down to a fairly agreeable, though basically boring, routine. Up at the crack of pseudo-dawn. Breakfast of plasticized hardtack, ersatz salt pork and imitation artificial coffee. Clean up parrot droppings. Manure hydroponics. Dust free-fall bowling trophies. Lunch of hardtack, salt pork and coffee and a bottle of rum. Vomit. Clean up parrot droppings. Manure hydroponics. Mop the decks and press the button that activated the death ray that cleaned the heads. After first checking they weren't occupied since the captain took a dim view of him death-raying the crew. Take navigational reading and help Rick plot new navigational course according to Rand McNally's GUIDE TO POSSIBLE COORDINATES OF FABLED STARSHIP PORTS. Feed super-hamsters that powered the star-drivers. Dinner of hardtack, salt pork, coffee with artificial sweetener substitute, then two bottles of rum and the juice of one lime to add some flavor and to prevent space scurvy. Recreation hour. Tell dirty stories. Curse. Vomit. Pass out. Just like back in the Troopers.

Most certainly, though Bill cherished the highly challenging and rewarding vocation of Guano Engineering, and the rum was nice (even though he strongly suspected that it was dehydrated alcohol and rum essence that Rick mixed with tap water in the kitchen), it was the recreation hour that Bill enjoyed the most. During this time, he and Rick could swap stories, or Archimedes and Rick would put on what they thought were their hilarious comedy schticks and soft shoe routines, which bored Bill so tremendously that he would fall asleep if he even thought about them. At least when their act ended Bill was free to read or watch Rick's huge supply of alien pornography (he particularly enjoyed THE MATING FROLIC OF THE SEVEN VENUSIAN SEXES which appeared to be a combination of a complicated orgy and SWAN LAKE).

However, as placid as life was in this Quest for the Holy Bar and Grill, he had to come to the conclusion that there something definitely *unreal* about it. Ever since Bruce the satyr had dragged him into the ocean things had been just a shade less than substantial. Oh, the first bit with Irma and the Fields of Elysium, the Furries and the climb up the mountain had all *seemed* real enough. He'd seen, felt, tasted, heard and smelt the usual wash of sensations. He'd performed the usual bodily functions with the usual enthusiasm, or lack of it, had drunk and lusted with the exact same urgency and specifics that had imbued his farmboy days and his Trooper career. And while in a normal human life, admittedly it *was* rather odd to meet up with mythological creatures, get a dead dove slung around your neck, then go gallivanting after your lady love in a starship named DESIRE with a possibly immortal hero and his neurotic parrot, Bill had, in his brief lifetime which he hoped to extend, experienced unusual adventures in a number of exotic and nauseating places. (Which are chronicled in a number of exciting volumes all available at the outlet where you bought this book.) He took it all in stride.

However, from time to time, he would catch glimpses of disquieting unsolidity in his peripheral vision. Nothingness. Blankness. Nada. Tabula rasa. He'd swing his head around quickly, and whatever was *supposed* to be there, be it control board, dope dispenser, ersatz imitation food-substitute machine, dehydrated water-closet, parrot, Rick—suddenly *was* there. But only after a subliminal blur, a shuffling of the air, like a suggestion of a quick Tri-Dee dissolve or an acute hangover.

Since what rum he could keep down generally kept Bill numb enough to not care much (although in truth rum was soon knocked off his list of top ten alcoholic drinks, and he yearned for their arrival at the Holy Bar and Grill if only to drink his fill of *other* potables) what happened one morning was particularly upsetting. Yawning and blinking and wishing that the word *rum* would be permanently stricken from his memory banks, he noticed after awhile that he was having a hard time sealing up his space boots. Or rather he wasn't sealing up his space boots because he wasn't closing the seals. He could not close the seals because the stumps of his arms could not do the job because his hands were missing.

The wild frantic screaming and fits of panic woke up Captain Rick and his parrot soon enough. Yawning, Rick the Supernal Hero raced down to see what the fuss was about, wearing only his galactic Dr. Dentons and a yawn, Archimedes in full flap behind him.

"My hands!" Bill shrieked incontinently. "They're gone!"

Since Bill was waving his arms in the air and running hysterically around the room, thoroughly panicked, Captain Rick quickly realized that something was wrong.

"Oh by Heavens! Has the venereal scurvy struck again! Have you been touching something that you should not have been touching, you naughty Trooper. Here, let's have a look!" Rick ordered, placing a monocle over his good eye.

Quivering and shaking with this most frightful trauma that can be visited upon a Trooper, eyes averted, Bill slowly and reluctantly extended the stumps of his arms.

"Awwwwwk!" screeched the parrot, horrified at all

the screaming and raw emotion. Somehow, it managed to hide its eyes with its wings.

"Well, I must say, this is a tempest in a teapot. Or something to do with the fickle finger of fate. There is, I am forced to say, no signs of disintegration, and certainly none of disappearance."

Baffled, Bill opened reluctant eyes and looked at his wrists. Hands. Two. Both in place.

"What kind of bowb is this?!" Bill howled in relief. "What's wrong with me? I'm going mad, I tell you, mad!"

"Let us do try not to overdramatize this late at night."

"Yes, I'm sorry." Bill's teeth chattered as he explained to Captain Rick the feelings of unreality he'd been experiencing lately. Since Bill was particularly frazzled and looked as though he wasn't going to get much sleep that night, Captain Rick treated him to a glass of warm soy milk with honey and mustard and rum. Guaranteed to cure anything. Or at least to take your mind off your troubles as you retched your guts out. It was a measure of Bill's distraction that he actually ingested the atrocious concoction and held his glass out for seconds.

"Arrrrr!" Captain Rick agreed, shaking his long locks. "I know what you mean, mate. I get that feeling from time to time meself. It's a strange life, it is. I'm just hoping I get me answers to me questions that have haunted me lo! these many years at the Holy Bar and Grill."

"Questions. What are your questions?"

"Why, the eternal questions of the Philosophers, of course, Bill me lad. The riddles that have haunted mankind since the ancient days, e'en before distilling was invented, which must have meant a pretty grim world.

"Namely, who came first, flying saucers or Raymond Palmer. Or, its logical corollary, did Raymond Palmer come from a Flying Saucer?

"Two, which came first, the chicken or the Western Omelette with home fries on the side?

"Three, if a tree falls in the woods, and there's no one there to hear it, does it fall upwards or downwards. And *its* corollary, if a deaf man falls in the wood, does he make a sound?"

"Four, does God exist, and if he (or she) does why does drinking too much eventually kill you, why does sex produce disease and finally why can I never get good tickets for the Galactic World Series?"

"And finally, Bill, the real stumper, what is the meaning of life, why is a man born, why does he live, and why does he die—and where the hell can I get a good bottle of Pepto Abysmal for Archimedes. I'm getting sick of the smell of parrot bowb all over the place."

Bill's head reeled at the depth of these philosophical questions. Incredible! Profound! It was all too much for him, so he asked for another soy milk and pyech to obfuscate the implications aborning in his head.

To relax him further, Captain Rick told him his story.

CAPTAIN RICK'S TALE
or
"Stars in My Handkerchief Like Clumps of Green Gunk"

to unwind the digital alarm clock.

So ginsberged out for the universe to give him a moniker.

The sub-voice answered with an eructation.

Belched forth the answer: Kid, you sniveling cyberrunt bratshit, what the bowb do I care? Captain Kid, Captain Rick, career astronauts and beats with bongos pound and sound forth the international anthems, and sheesh! the price of bananas in Nicaragua has skyrocketed, and elevator operators grease their asses with their thumbs, and Walden's and Dalton's are really down on Pynchon-hitters lately, so what why should I give a good Gesundheit? Anyway, I got this mouthful of cold espresso in my mouth, and hell if I know why? Jesus! Ptoui! Tastes *dreadful!*

Another minute Kid squatted on the Johnny-on-the-Spot, clutching his New York Review of Books and Little Magazine toilet paper, listening to his heaving breath and kerouac inner-music.

Beyond leafy trees, moonlight painted, wallpapered and interior decorated strips of fashionable West Village light in the forest.

He rubbed poetry across his bum. Somewhere in Soho (or maybe Tribeca) an art gallery opens a William Burroughs shotgun art show. The whole city has turned into skyscraper after skyscraper of art galleries in this fiction-turned-semirealscape of stranger-than-real gangs wandering inanely about with holograms for switchblades.

The leaves leered and winked.

The woman wearing a sweatshirt of shadows and a Jimi Hendrix hairdo rose up from the dark culture of Sixties and smell of hashish. A pill of light lay upon her nose.

Captain Kid and the woman had sex, and then tried to figure out what would happen in the eight hundred and seventy-seven page anticlimax.

For what is "Myth" but the neo-deconstructionist prose of a missing literary critic who lisps?

"Huh?" said Bill, quite baffled.

"Oh, sorry, that's the highbrow version for my intellectual friends at cocktail parties," said Captain Rick. "I dare say you want something more soothing. Arrrrrrr. Yes, I have just the thing."

Rick rolled out his thousand watt amplifier as big as a space tug, his Stratosphere-blaster electro-drone guitar. He laid down a few tasteful deady-metal fret licks (deady-metal being the au courant fashionable version of rock-and-roll, where computer-operated corpses of electrocuted murderers fronted your standard lead guitar, kitchen synth, drum and bass ensemble) and began to sing.

Archimedes squawked and, in a hail of feathers and a critical splatter of fresh doo-doo, fled the room.

CAPTAIN RICK'S STORY
TAKE TWO
"Ballad of the Supernal Hero"

They call me the Hero with a Thousand Faces.
I see lots of things and go lots of places.
I'm a mythic hero, I like to ramble.
But *my* hero's not Joseph but John W. Campbell.

Ye see, sometimes I'm a pirate, sometimes a saint,
But first a homo sapiens; coward I ain't.
Mankind was meant to rule all these stars
Build malls and condos, and taverns and bars.

As I child I was a wimp, I found nothing arousing.
Till I read John on Dean Drive and Dowsing.
Now I travel from planet to planet, circum-celestial
Killing things smart and extraterrestial.

"Terra Uber-alles" I sing with a belch and a shout
And my surging male humanity I like to flout.
And when things get grim, and bare goes the
   cupboard
I just pull out DIANETICS by good old Ron
   Hubbard.

My greatest adventure. Hmm, well, let me see.
There was the time in a cantina that I had to wee
Alas, I'd left my blaster in my digital locker
There in the stall was Lay-ya and Luke Starfokker.

Now Lay-ya I'd divorced 'couple years before
Sex with a princess was mostly a bore.
Luke I thought was raising sheep on Mount Shasta.
"Help!" Luke cried. "We need you and your blaster!"

"Lord Brain-Death is back, the Farce help us all.
We hear Heavy Breathing, and that is his Call.

He's back from the dead, practicing evil Craft
I am scared, I am crazy—I'm going half daft."

No sooner said, that, than Storm Troopers attacked.
Dodging deathrays, quickly, to the DESIRE we
    backed.
We zoomed through space, hid in nebulean bogs.
Trained hard for the battle, read old ANALOGS.

Good old John Campbell, his essays were
    profounding!
Hectoring lectures in the good old ASTOUNDING.
In those pre-Spielberg days you'll have to agree
John would have crunched the ALIEN, barfed on ET.

"Bowb the Force," he'd have said, "Man the garrison!
Technology rules! Up Anderson! Up Harrison!
Alien invasion? Build a great gun!
Stay to the Right of Baen and Attila the Hun."

So we cobbled and soldered like technology's fools
A better death ray, using brains and slide rules!
John would've liked it, Doc Smith would turn green
Buddy, this beamer was big, huge, and obscene!

So we hurtled on out to meet the death fleet
A terrible sight—they were something to meet!
A thousand alien ships, designed by George Lucas
Wanted to turn us to slag and horrible mucus.

"Surrender to the Dark Side," said Death, big
    surprise!
"Join the Empire! Make mythic movies!
    Merchandise!"
In answer we just aimed our out big beamer and
    happily shot 'em
No way was John's boys gonna kiss the Empire's
    bottom.

Now, for Brain Death technology was a given!
But his scientists hadn't read Tom Clancy, Pournelle
    and Niven

ASF's sons, all—so what if they couldn't write.
They knew their nuts from their bolts, and boy could
    they fight.

Our blaster, you see, wasn't loaded with energy
    rounds.
It was stocked with ultra and hyperfrequency sounds.
Homocentric readings from Asimov, deCamp and
    Clement.
Dickson and del Rey, thrilling as drying cement.

We blasted the coup de grace! Hyperboreals!
John W. Campbell's editorials!
Stunned, the Empire's death ships whimpered away.
Old Death hoisted surrender. Ours was the day!

They say good old John Campbell, he's somewhere
    up there.
Watching new writers with all their hot air.
Gulping aloud great celestial gulps.
"If this junk is SF—then bring back the pulps!"

The last chords of the song hung in the air between
them like the final strains of Bill's favorite martial music
by John Philip Soused. Big fat tears dripped down his
cheeks. He sniffled and choked back his heart rising in
his throat.

"Bowb! That. . . . that was the most beautiful song
. . . I . . . I *ever* heard in my entire life."

"Then you will be feeling better, First Mate Bill?"

"Yeah! Much better."

"Arrrrrr! That's me hearty! You're a super trooper,
Bill. Arrrrr! It's a pleasure having you aboard. Now we
better get back to our hammocks and squeeze in the
winks! Navigational computer says that the Holy Bar
and Grill is just a matter of days away!"

Irma! He would be able to see Irma again. He sighed
with passion like a leaking locomotive. Smiling happily
at the thought of her bright innocent eyes, her shapely

body, her gentle feminine sighs.

He fell asleep then, still smiling. Dreaming dreams of such erotic content that his body temperature rose five degrees and moisture condensed on the bulkhead above.

CHAPTER **8**

LAST CALL AT THE
HOLY BAR AND GRILL

AS IT HAPPENED, IT TOOK SOMEWHAT MORE
than a week to finally find their goal, and Rick the
Supernal Hero had to resort to a variation of the Bloater
Drive he'd bought in a used starship lot, called a Bilious
Drive. Bill had always hated the Bloater Drive when
Empire Trooper ships had used it to hop between star
systems and if anything the Bilious Drive was exceed-
ingly worse, since it involved pumping the entire space
ship full of a singularly repulsive mixture of xenon and
hydrogen and sulfurous gases which made everything—
if the Bible is to be believed—literally stink like hell.
When the right mixture of gases had been reached, their
molecules were vibrated electronically until the gas, the
ship and all of its contents were shaking like crazy and

synchronized with the atomic pulse beat of their destination. The instant this occurred everything would be belched across the cosmic distances in a most uncomfortable and sickening manner. Bill even thought good things about the Bloater Drive when this happened.

But when the starship named DESIRE finally drifted into the Ad Hoc System, he saw the gigantic neon signs flashing out the letters "Holy Bar and Grill," "On the Sands Stage: Mr. Wayne Newton!" and "Nude Drinking" and "Topless-Bottomless Bar" which he hoped meant more nudity and not prefrontal lobotomy and gluteotomy. A tear in his eye, a frog in his throat—and incipient liver failure on the horizon—Bill knew that his heart had finally found a home.

The Holy Bar and Grill was actually a large complex of hover-buildings, squatting beatifically in a bank of chartreuse clouds on anti-grav plates, high above the giant methane world of Zeus.

"Old Zeus loves this huge planet mostly because it's named after him," explained Rick as he swung the starship named DESIRE in to land it on a pillar of crimson flame.

"Yikes," said Bill. "How come there's a pillar of crimson flame down there in the middle of that spaceport?"

"Complimentary ionized starship hull cleaning service!"

"We're going to *cook*!"

"Also kills any space bacteria hanging onto the fins. Asteroid barnacles and such. Don't worry, Bill. It's perfectly harmless."

Later, after their burns were treated and the roasted Archimedes, who had fired his last guanic salvo, was served up in sandwiches as a thank you to the white-robed medics who had treated them, Rick allowed that he had forgotten you were supposed to turn up the air

conditioning a tad when landing in the Holy Pillar of
Starship Cleaning Flame. Bill took it all in stride. Cleaning up parrot bowb wasn't too bad, but Archimedes'
constant stream of knock-knock jokes was beginning to
set his teeth on edge. It was a pleasure to realize that he
would never have to listen again to the like of "Knock-
knock," "Who's there?," "Toby," "Toby who?"
"Toby or not Toby."

And he was really looking forward to a nice cold beer!

The Holy Bar and Grill was the biggest drinking saloon Bill had ever seen. After they checked into their
room at the overpriced and undercleaned Hiltom Hotel,
they walked past banks upon banks upon banks of slot
machines, blackjack tables and Galactic lottery booths.
Bill was stunned. The bar in the main building stretched
for over two miles and there were clouds obscuring the
far end. It was lined with an army of cloned android
bartenders, all of whom looked equally repulsive, with
pig's heads—which had a tendency to drool down their
tusks—and twelve-fingered hands which were great for
carrying a lot of glasses at once.

The lines of taps served every beer in the known
universe, from Old Peculier from a planet called En-
gland to Really Old and a Lot More Peculier from Ire-
land, along with Happy Barrel Dredgings from New
South Whales. Lines of all manner of bottled spirits
strung out like colorful baubles on a giant prostrate
Christmas tree stretching for kilometers and kilometers.
Bill was alternately assailed by whiffs and fumes of blissful brews, scintillating spirits. Oh, heady hops! Oh,
mischievous malts, ah! the blissful joys of alcohol! He
had the sudden thought that maybe in this place even
the bar-rags probably tasted good, but resisted the sudden impulse to find out.

In mundane matters like women and the Troopers,
Bill was simply a knee jerk, reflex kind of guy with any
traces of conscience or original thought eroded away by

years of military indoctrination. But in matters of drinking, he often waxed philosophical since this, and creative cursing, were the only areas of originality the Troopers had left open to him. Why, some pundit had asked recently, when there are *numerous* varieties of mood and mind-altering drugs available these days, naturally from exotic worlds, or synthetically from legal or illegal laboratories, why is the favored drug amongst the military, and perhaps even the human universe—alcohol in all its insidious forms?

To this question, Bill had three relevant responses:

1. Alcohol gets you drunk.
2. Alcohol then gets you even drunker.
3. Alcohol then gets you unconscious, which is the only escape from the military a Lifer would ever get.

But, continued the pundit's challenge, why alcohol when there are so many other inebriating drugs that were less addictive, that did not cause eventual gross tissue damage in the internal organs, that did not have such a history of human degradation, suffering and shame permanently affixed to all their various and sundry forms?

Bill might have pointed out that perhaps there was a natural need in a human being to get blotto from time to time; but he was only aware of this instinctually and could not articulate the thought or the urge. He might have sung the praises for the panorama of taste available in the wide range of alcoholic drinkables, but since most of his favorite drinks tasted awful and since by the third or fourth drink he didn't taste anything anyway, he didn't.

As it happened, one day in the misty past in a low bar on Boozeworld, a Trooper R & R center, Bill was enthusiastically sitting, enjoying a couple dozen drinks and heading quickly for alcoholic extinction while ogling the multiple pink mammaries of the whorebots, the entertainment the planet provided, when a temperance-minded missionary, transported there by the authorities as some sort of sadistic joke, supremely disgusted by the activities of his fellow humans at the bar, brought up these very same arguments to Bill and asked him why, in light of all knowledge of the evils of drink, he was ruining himself with demon liquor.

Bill had remembered saying, with great drunken clarity and understanding, "Because I can feel it doing me harm." Not satisfied, the missionary had pressed for a more intelligent explanation so that Bill, too drunk to expound at length, and physically incapable of shlurring more than the shimplest shentence, summed all up in a brilliant Cartesian sentence:

"I drink, therefore I am."

He had then added a certain pungent punctuation to his remarks by flipping his cookies all over the missionary before mercifully passing out.

But the philosophy stuck, and so did the philosophical wax, so now as he surveyed this dipsomaniac Disneyland, spread out before him like a feast of unreason, he 'am'ed with every core of his being, much as Zoroastrian monks 'om'ed with theirs.

"Finally! Finally, I have reached my goal," said Rick, the Supernal Hero, falling upon his knees with awe. "Throughout the universe I have searched for one particular beer! And here is the Holy Bar and Grill, which surely serves every potation concocted in the Universe! A bar of truly mythic proportions!" He struggled up to his feet, stumbled toward a clearing in the shiny waxed wood. "Arrrrrrr! C'mon, first mate. This one's on me!"

Bill, never one to refuse a free drink, followed his Captain. But at the same time he surveyed with growing gloom the crowds milling through the huge bar. How ever was he going to find Irma in *this* place?

"Bartender!" called out Rick. "Set up a round for me and my buddy."

"What's your poison, fella?" said the bartender with asinine enthusiasm at the stupid line.

"Holy Grail Stout!" said Rick with a broad grin as

he slapped his Gold Galactic cred voucher on the walnut surface of the bar.

All drinkers within earshot stopped talking, stopped drinking, seemed to even stop breathing. They turned and stared at the newcomer and the bartender.

"Sorry, stranger," lisped the bartender in an unctuous androidal voice. "That's the one brew we don't have."

Rick blinked. "Well, then, how about some Holy Grail ale?"

"Sorry. Don't have that either."

"Uhmm. Well, then, what about Holy Grail *lager*."

"Nope."

"Holy Grail pilsner?"

"Uh uh."

Rick, by this time, had turned quite white. "Arrrrrrr! But I've traveled parsecs upon parsecs to slake this special thirst. I was told that the Holy Bar and Grill served *every* drink known to mankind!"

"We do. Everything but the Holy Grail line. Nobody knows where that stuff is, though we've had plenty of Sir Galahads and Sir Reptitious like you traipsing through looking for it. How about a nice Aldebaran Moosetail bitter? I personally can vouch you'll not find a better brew south of the North Star!"

The crestfallen Rick muttered gloomily, "No way. I am going to need something a lot stronger than that to kill the growing state of depression that is about to overwhelm me. Two Dickhead whiskeys, bartender. That is two barrels. And you'd better serve them in pint mugs."

That sounded good to Bill. *Anything* but rum. He accepted his Dickhead mug, needed both hands to lift it, and with uncharacteristic reserve, merely sipped it as he surveyed the room. That is, after he had half-drained it to see if it had gone off in the barrel. Still no sign of Irma. And thankfully no sight either of gentlemen walking about carrying thunderbolts in their hands, as Zeus was reputed to do.

However, parts of the room *were* peripherally fading in and out. That damnable problem with his grip on reality again! Maybe this huge room held too much for his tiny brain to absorb, thought Bill. By the end of the Dickhead jug, however, and the beginning of the next, things were fading in and out even more, but by this time Bill really didn't care.

Finally, after the second barrel was well gotten into and he was feeling decidedly squiffed, the man parked at the bar beside them tapped him on the shoulder. "Oy, mate!" he said, staring at him through bottle-bottom glasses. "What's that 'anging 'round yer neck there?"

Bill had become so accustomed to his little item of deceased avian jewelry since the "loo stasis" had been sprayed on, stopping the stench, that he'd almost forgotten about it.

"This," he said, watching as a fly was zapped in the static electronic field, ". . . this is a dead dove. Quiet, though, pal. Don't call attention. Everybody will want one too."

The interruption, however, had succeeded in knocking Bill out of his alcoholic reverie and slightly back on course. He remembered the main reason he was here at the Holy Bar and Grill.

"Irma!" he cried aloud, turning and frantically shaking his companion's arm. "Captain Rick, do you zhee Irma anywhere hereaboutsabouts?"

Captain Rick, dejected and depressed, was just working his way towards the bottom of the whiskey barrel, mumbling to himself about searching for Holy Grail beer until the day he died. "Irma?" he said, eyelids at half-mast, trying to get Bill in focus. "Just find Zeus, man. When you find Zeus, you'll find Irma."

"Zeus? But how the bowb am I going to find Zeus?" Bill said. "There must be hundreds of thousands of people in this place."

"Who's looking for people?" Rick cackled incontinently. "You're looking for a god."

"Zeus?" said the neighbor. "You looking for the Great God Zeus? Why didn't you say so, mate? I just passed the bugger coming back from a celestial slash down in the Netherzone Quadrant. He's got 'imself a private party going down there."

"Netherzone Quadrant?" said Bill, his excitement at the thought of finding Irma sobering him slightly. "Where's that?"

"Like I said, it's down by the WCs! The Bogs, Jakes—or whatever you call them in your dialect." The mustachioed gentleman pointed over to the side of the hall, where four signs were posted. No writing on them, just Intergalactic symbols. One sign depicted a man, another what was probably a woman. Bill blinked at them rapidly until he could make them out. Men's and ladies' room he guessed. The adjoining sign depicted a six-limbed chitinous creature. Alien's room. The last was the largest, and it showed a huge halo parked by a toilet.

Gods' room.

"Rick, I'm going down to find Irma," said Bill.

"Go 'head. Arrrr. I'm not going anywhere." And, in the endless quest for alcoholic companionship, misery and drunkenness love sympathy, he bought the neighbor a drink, and together they toasted the dead and much-missed Archimedes the parrot.

Bill, who missed the feathery farter not at all, indeed had his own dead bird to consider, did not join in. He headed for the toilet signs, and there took a pneumatic tube to the Netherzone Quadrant. After visiting the men's room successfully, he emerged back into the long corridor. He only had to walk a very short distance to hear the thunder and booming of Zeus' party.

Roaring big band music filled the air as he opened the door and was confronted by the vast and twisted alien Escher print panorama of the Netherzone Room. Apparently, Zeus had twisted gravitational effects in such pretzel forms that in one part of the huge room, people were standing on the ceiling, and in four others, people were standing on the walls. As for the big band—well, that multitudinous ensemble hung swaying in a crescent moon suspended in the very middle of the room. They were doing a heated version of an ear-destroying number that had the walls throbbing in and out. Suddenly, as Bill walked into the wash of music and art-wrecko atmosphere, his mood foot started twitching and spasming, moving about in time to the beat.

The hairy-hoofed thing was trying to *dance*!

"That's '*Satin* Doll' they're playing, idiot! Not *Satyr's* Doll!"

However, the foot ignored him, and he had to prance about a little as he moved about the roomscape, searching for Zeus and his lost true love, the incredibly luscious and lost Irma!

It did not take long to find Zeus. The God was on the ceiling, sitting at a long table crowded with a cornucopia of contraband.

CHAPTER 9

MIND-MASTERS OF THE OVER-GLAND

IN A THOROUGHLY FOUL MOOD, MORE SEX-
ually frustrated than he'd ever felt in his entire life, Bill
opened gummy lids and reached up to scratch the top
of his head. He felt the fumbling resistance of wires. He
heard a popping, a squealing—machine sounds rumbled
all around him like amplified soap bubbles. Squeaks and
blips and hollow "pings" echoed metallically and plast-
ically.

"He's waking up again! Is that wise, Doctor?" said a
familiar voice.

"Yes. His unconsciousness has fueled the Matrix suf-
ficiently," said another familiar voice.

Bill groaned. He lifted his head, looking around him.
Again the resistance of the wires. He could feel cold

metal now, adhering to the skin on his forehead. He
could feel tiny subcutaneous implants in his scalp. He
could feel the needle of a drug-drip, intravenously
feeding him the contents of an upended bottle labeled
with a skull and crossbones. He felt like a sliced-open
body that had been poorly stitched together. He felt for
the very first time in his life like a beetle pinned down
by a long pin through his thorax. Felt this way even
though he knew that he didn't have a thorax. The room
swam before him, a thing that rooms usually find it very
hard to do. Vaguely he could see a form in front of him.
The figure wore a white lab coat, glasses and a steth-
oscope. Bill suddenly smelled the familiar scent of antiseptics.

A doctor? Antiseptics? Was he back in the hospital
then? Fragments of memory swam about him like
chunks of detritus from an explosion, floating in free
fall. Vague images of Bruce the satyr . . . the Fields of
Elysium . . . delicious wine . . . the droppings of Archimedes the parrot. . . .

Irma's smiling face.

"Irma!" he cried again, struggling in his containment.

"Whoa there, Trooper. Settle down, big fellow," said
the unctuously theoretically comforting voice of the
doctor, leaning over him. Bill looked up and the vague
form resolved into recognizable features. The nasty,
pointy nose, the gruesome chin, the furtive look in those
bulging eyes. . . .

"Where am I?"

"You're in a secret compound, deep below the reefs
of the ocean on Colostomy IV, Bill. You're here on the
most important and monumentous mission of your career as a human being."

Bill looked harder. That voice, that face!

"Dr. Delazny!"

"That's right, Bill. Now calm down. No one's going
to hurt you!"

"Secret compound? *Whose* secret compound?"

"Gee, Bill!" a little voice piped up. He was aware of the scampering of tiny reptilian feet up the metal gurney top. A heavy weight suddenly landed on his chest. He craned his neck and was suddenly eyeballs to eyeballs with a seven-inch tall lizard with four arms. "Don't you know? Haven't you figured it out yet, buddy?"

A Chinger!

More than that, he recognized the high-pitched, adenoidal voice he had come to detest more than the ghost of Sergeant Deathwish Drang, who from time to time haunted his drugged dreams.

It was Eager Beager!

"Eager Beager!" said Bill. "I thought you were dead."

"The rumors of my death were pure hyperbole, Bill! You like that word Bill? 'Hyperbole!' Yeah. But Eager Beager no longer. He was just a humanoid robot that I operated from a control where his brain would be if he had a brain. My name is Bgr the Chinger, as you should remember but you have forgot with all the brain-stirring. I am the Chinger specialist in alien life forms—and gee, humans are as alien as they come, let me tell you!—I've been doing a little study into human semiotics, human literary terms, and of course, in-depth human psychology. Gee—I got lots of new terms for you. Can you say 'phenomenological psycho-metascape?' Gee—I didn't think so."

Mostly, Bill was just laboring to breathe. Being from a ten-G (hence perhaps his preoccupations with the expression "gee") world, although they were small, the Chingers were also very dense and very, *very* heavy. "Could—you—get—off, Eager?"

"Gee—oh yeah. Sure, Bill. We got a lot to talk about." The Chinger hopped down to the gurney again, capered over to sit beside Bill's face, its little tail wiggling with reptilian happiness. "Yeah. Like, soldiers, how's the subversion of the Empire going? The dissemination of truth, peace and righteousness?"

"Death to all Chingers!" growled Bill.

"Hmm. I thought so. A backslider. I thought we had a deal, Bill. Or maybe your training was just too much. Gee—too bad!"

Bill turned to Dr. Latex Delazny. Slowly, the truth began to filter through his thick head. "I'm being held captive in a Chinger compound. Which means—" He snarled at the Doctor, bearing his fangs. "You're a Chinger spy, Doctor. You're a traitor!"

The thin man stood erect to his full height, puffing out his chest with hurt pride. "I am nothing of the sort! I am a humanitarian! I work for the best interests of the human race. I work for armistice in the Empire-Chinger War. I work for peace, goodness, happiness! I work to cure the aberrations of the human subconscious!"

"Traitor scum! And I trusted you with my foot? Where have you taken me? What's going on?"

"Gee—and it is a nice foot, isn't it Bill?" said Bgr, scampering down to admire the cloven hoof.

Bill remembered. "Yeah! A 'mood foot' the Doctor calls it. And it's your fault, Bgr!"

"Knock it off, Bill. Shut up and listen. The Doctor has a lecture for you. We're going to need you for the next phase of the operation. Gee—and this is going to be fun, too!"

"Not really a lecture—rather an attempt to impart information, always a difficult task. Particularly with you. Try to understand that your subconscious must share the group subconscious which is a hell of a lot smarter than your conscious mind. Which is not saying very much in any case. What you experienced truly *happened*, though perhaps not quite in the same dimensional-experiential plane we are accustomed to."

"Does what you say mean that I'm still cursed with the Grime of the Aging Marinator!" Bill moaned. Feeling at some deep subliminal level the thong that went straight through his neck, that was attached to a lot of really vital stuff. "Arrrrrrgh!" he observed.

"You must be positive about the situation, Bill. You

have also met the love of your life, the woman of your dreams. . . . And she truly exists, if you allow her to!"

"Wushha?" Bill commented incoherently, about all the communication he was up to at the moment. Delazny nodded benignly, feeling that he was finally establishing communication, albeit at a very primitive level.

"You got it, baby! Irma, of course! The beautiful Irma!" He gestured toward the machines. "She's waiting for you back in the paradigm construct, Bill. And if you find her, the power of your developing mental capabilities might actually give her physical existence in *this* plane, just as that dead dove hanging around your neck has attained a reality of existence here."

"Irma!" Bill remembered! He remembered Irma's lovely smile, the gorgeous curves of her lissome body, the delightful smell of her perfumed underarms! An EKG needle suddenly started bleeping with alarm. A hormonal count needle nearby suddenly swung so hard into the red, it busted off and flopped onto the floor.

Bgr's bug eyes managed to bug out even further than normal. "Gee!" was all the Chinger could say.

Dr. Delazny smiled smugly. Another curious expression crossed his face at the mention of Irma, as though he recognized the name, but he was veiling his thoughts on the subject. "You see, Bgr? I told you about the astonishing power exercised when in the strange human combination of hormones and psychic energy in our species called 'love.'" He turned back to his patient. "You can be with Irma again if you like, Bill. You can even bring her back here. But first you have to find her."

The very thought of her melted Bill's heart; a sort of amorous coronoid. Irma! Darling Irma. More than ever, more than anything, She was his heart's desire. More than being a Technical Fertilizer Operator, more than owning a whiskey distillery on Hopworld, more than getting a new liver, more even than finally getting a normal human foot sewn onto his leg.

Irma!

"How do I find her, Doc?" he slobbered salivically, his eyes glazing over with love.

"Very simple, my boy. You see that so far we've been experimenting merely with your consciousness, sending it out into our paradigm construct. You were specifically chosen because of your very strong spermataphoric functions. So strong that they appear to overpower the conscious powers of the mind. You see, in short, Bill, the Chingers and I believe we have determined the truth about human beings, and why they wage war so much. Human beings, Bill, think not with their brains so much as with their gonads. Since culturally the Empire is basically male-dominated, the primary human emotion that governs it is *sex*. Particularly *aggressive* sex. Now, here's where the human brain comes in. Unfortunately for Chingers and the rest of the universe, human females are not mindless bovines. They are not really basically interested in the mindless and random promiscuous copulation that all human males want, deep down in their musty hearts no matter how much they intellectually deny it. In fact, the female of the species is far smarter than the male. But, alas, they too are riddled with hormones—albeit most of them far more Byzantine than pure testosterone—which creates a muddled soup of their reasoning abilities, and thus quite odd, albeit complex, little entities who don't really know what they want on any level, but work fiendishly hard to get it. Since the males can't get constant, raw sex they must channel their aggression elsewhere. Hence, war. Hence domination of the universe—"

"Including unwarranted aggression upon us peace-loving Chingers!" said Eager Beager.

"Exactly. I seek understanding of humanity, Bill. But more than that, I seek to venture into the very core of the human brain, to tap the collective energy of mankind, the Over-Gland if you will, and perhaps make some minor evolutionary adjustments!"

"Right on, baby!" piped up Bgr. "Like maybe cut down on the hormone flow. Volume down human aggressive instincts! Make the galaxy safe for the peace-loving races. Maybe then the Empire will stop shooting long enough to realize that the Chingers want peace in the Universe, and the only reason we're fighting is so we're not the 102,324th species that you blood-thirsty creatures have rendered extinct!"

Bill frowned. "Wait a minute. Let me get this straight. What this amounts to is a kind of collective desexing of mankind. You want to geld the human race! You filthy rotten Chingers! And you, you lousy bowing traitor Doctor!" Bill frothed and writhed on the table, as the hormonally fomented tides of macho bullshit coursed through his cerebellum.

Dr. Delazny shook his head fervently. "Oh no, Bill. Emasculation is the wrong analogy. We merely wish to halve the aggressive impulses of mankind—and by finding their root in the Over-Gland, we believe we can do just that. And we've chosen *you* to do it. Look at it this way. Every male has got a throbbing, pulsating sex drive, right? So what harm would it do if every male had that drive reduced by half? Life would go on as before. Lovers would love and babies would be born. Only with that weensy bit of aggression removed maybe we could stop war and killing and wasting everything in sight. Not a bad idea, wouldn't you admit?"

"Not a bad idea!?" Bill frothed. "It is the stupidest thing I have heard since I was asked to volunteer to reenlist. Racial glandular castration!" The thought of giving up some small iota of his macho image so enraged Bill that his mind worked overtime. He suddenly felt himself charged with righteousness, and an unusual oratory elegance.

"No way, you sadistic sawbones. How could I allow that to happen to the human race? How can I remove, even partly, the source of the great achievements of

humankind! From these instincts came the urge to sail
the oceans of a thousand ancient planets, to climb mountains, to discipline the very elements into obedience.
From these so-called hormonal aggressive instincts arose
the desire to risk getting blown up in primitive spacecraft
to conquer the planets of the solar system, and then
venture out into the galaxy! You request that I betray
the source of power that has given my noble race such
vision, such ambitions, such imagination, such splendid
dreams, such fertile karma?"

"Bill! Start thinking with your brain not with your
ductless glands! We'll install you and Irma on a nice little
planet where you can be a Technical Fertilizer Operator
and drink to your heart's content, free too. No more
war. No more Troopers, Bill. Oh, and we'll get that
dead dove off your neck. And lastly, we'll give you the
most marvelous *foot*, perfectly cultured from an expen-
sive foot vat!"

Bill instantly forgot the racial ramifications of the plan
and substituted selfishness and a quick profit in their
place. "Okay. What do I have to do?"

"I told you the new foot would be the clincher, Doc!"
said Bgr. "Let's see if we can get this ponging pigeon
off him, and wheel him into the changing room!"

CHAPTER 10

A ROLE OF THE DICE!

BILL STOOD IN FRONT OF THE FULL-LENGTH mirror, jaw gaping as he bulged his eyes at his reflection.

"What's with this? Why the crummy outfit and haircut?" he demanded.

"Give him another drink from the wine-skin, Bruce," said Dr. Delazny, rummaging through piles of hats and garments. "You must relax, Bill. Drinky, drinky, don't say no."

The satyr robot (the very one who had kidnapped Bill on the ocean front and dragged him down to this top secret Chinger compound) capered forward, and unslung the large goat-skin drinking pouch from its neck. Bill, who had never refused a drink in his life, was horrified at the doc's suggestion, grabbed at the skin and shot a dark jet of the glutinous, resinous wine down his throat. Pretty poisonous stuff—but it contained alcohol! He smacked his lips and stared at himself again in the mirror.

A little better, but still weird as hell!

Bill was dressed in a long robe of sackcloth. Strapped to his feet were leather sandals. A wooden cross hung around his neck partially obscured by the dead dove that was still pendant there. A cowl was bunched up on his back, and he held a wooden staff in his hand. Electro-scissors and depilatory cream had made quick work of his hair—it was now in a tonsure.

Worst of all was his woolen underwear, which itched like a plague of crotch-crickets. He scratched industriously at all the irritated spots and looked over at Dr. Delazny, pawing through the pile of hats. He was depressed. Maybe this was better than lying on his back connected with a bunch of electrical equipment, but not much. "You wouldn't like to take the time to explain all this to me, would you, Doc? And what about the dove? You said you were getting rid of it?"

"In a moment . . . ah!" Doctor Delazny pulled out a hat from the pile. A skullcap, to be precise. He went to Bill and fitted it over his head. "This is really you. Sorry about the dove, impossible to remove at the present time. Now the good news, Bill, you are about to engage upon a quest."

"Not another quest!"

"Another one—and the most important one. In the land of the Over-Gland, all is metaphorical. Now that we have jelled it into semi-physical state, with your excellent help, of course, we can begin to look for the core. Once that is discovered, we can then take action to deal with the problems it represents. First, however, we have to find it. . . . Hence, the quest. So, we have developed a variation on a medieval game of Ancient Earth. A brief aberration of certain adolescents called 'role-playing games' developed somewhere in the dark ages before the planetary holocaust. Fortunately for mankind, the discovery was made that the playing of 'role-playing games,' schizophrenia, and signing blood pacts with Satan were all due to a lack of certain nutrients in the diet. The simple potato, *Solanum tuberosum*, proved to be rich in the minerals that could control this deficiency. Free Fry Kitchens were opened all across the world and soon adolescents were gorging themselves on this delicacy.

"The mental disease soon cleared up—and the manufacturers of Clearazits acne medicine grew rich. However, I have determined that by playing a variation of the 'role-playing' game involving a team of cooperating agents in dealing with the convoluted metaphorical highways and byways of the human Over-Gland, the inherent dangers may be overcome."

"A good chance," said Bgr the Chinger, popping out of the skull of Bruce the satyr. "Gee—at the very least one or two participants may actually get through!"

"A team. You mean that you two are coming along with me?"

Dr. Delazny shook his head. "Uhmm, no, we've got to stay back here at Chinger Central and monitor. However, we've assembled a crack group to travel with you, Bill.

"This game I've called 'Drunkards and Flagons.' You, Bill, have been assigned the role of the 'Drunken Monk.' Bgr, I think it's time that we let Bill keep the full wine-skin, don't you?"

"Gee—sure, you're the doctor."

The Chinger popped back inside the robot-skull and banged away at the controls, causing the robot to step forward and present Bill with the whole wine-skin. Bill took a grateful drink and then flung the thing over his shoulder. "A team, you say. You wouldn't like to tell me just who else is going?"

A roar suddenly vibrated the very structure of the room. A seven foot tall, shaggy blond man with a beard strode in, wearing furs, a sword and a cap from which protruded two horns. From one gorilla-sized hand hung a half-full bottle of Jack Spaniels whiskey. "Women! Where are the *women* you promised me!" he bellowed, sniffing the air as though to ferret out feminine pheromones.

"Bill, this is Ottar, an ancient Viking we discovered frozen in the Over-Gland. He will portray the Barbarian Hero role in the game." Delazny turned and gently held up a hand. "Plenty of women, Ottar. First, we make a movie, yes?"

Ottar's eyes glimmered with enthusiasm. Ottar grinned. "Ottar like movies. Ottar *movie star!*"

"Huh?" said Bill.

"Don't ask," said Bgr. There are some things best left unknown. He turned to Ottar in his satyr guise. "Remember Ottar. You find the Fountain of Hormones, and you'll also find your precious, darling Slithy Tove!"

Ottar grunted and grinned. Drool began to foam from his lips, beaded onto his food-encrusted beard. Bill was also aware of the profound stench the character was also giving off. Where was the "loo stasis" when he needed it?

"Okay, who else?" Bill asked with a sigh. He had thought about asking Ottar for a drink, but decided against it when he saw that the liquid in the bottle was green with pink foam on it.

"An old friend, Bill. Proof of the energy-to-matter efficacy of my equipment!" Dr. Delazny stepped over to a wall and pulled open a curtain. A man lay sprawled over a table, a stein of beer in one hand, a cutlass in another. Delazny prodded the man awake.

"It's Rick!" cried Bill, astonished. "Rick, the Supernal Hero!"

"Yes, but he'll be playing the role of the Virgin Knight in this particular adventure."

There were grating sounds as Rick opened his eyes. They were bright red and steaming slightly. He shud-

dered and clanked them shut, then took long and qua-
vering gulps of beer. This time he opened only one eye
a crack and blinked around him. His ruddy gaze fixed
on Bill and he said, "Arrrrr. Don't I know you, matey?"

Bill turned to Dr. Delazny. "And this is going to be
the team?" He took a drink and emitted a sound that
was somewhere between a sigh and a moan.

The other members of the motley crew were quickly
trotted out for introductions:

Clitoria, the Amazon warrior.

Hyperkinetic, the Trickster.

And finally, Missionary Position, the Cattlelick
Priest.

Ottar made a drunken lunge for Clitoria, but the seven
foot tall woman boxed his ears soundly, and knocked
him to the floor. "Try that again, you bushy bastard,
and I'll stick your whiskey bottle so far up your whatsit
that you'll need dynamite to get it out."

Hyperkinetic was dressed in gay colors and he carried
a lute, and had a despicable tendency to sing verses of
a long and dull marching song. In a nasal monotone:

"A questing we will go!
Summer, fall, or snow!
The Fountain of Hormones we must find.
So come on chaps—don't fall behind."

"Arrrr!" said Captain Rick. "I like this guy! Even
though he can't sing and his verse doesn't scan."

"Fountain of Hormones?" said Bill puzzled.

"Yes," said Doctor Delazny. "According to the best
of our readings in our computer, the goal of your quest
is called 'The Fountain of Hormones.' Exactly what that
means or exactly what it is has not yet been determined."

"But, gee—the name is pretty evocative though,"
said Bgr through his satyr guise.

The priest was a red-cheeked, merry-looking fellow,
who turned out to be the only volunteer on the Quest.

"Faith and begorrah!" he said when questioned by Bill on the subject. "And sure, sincerely I believe the lusts of the flesh so personified at the end of this quest are merely pagan heathen, and God willing I should like to bring them to the ways of righteousness."

"Arrrrr. Me, I don't give a bowb," said Rick. "Except for the fact I got a hot rumor that the Holy Brewery is right by the Fountain. The one that makes Holy Grail Stout. My soul thirsts after righteousness, but so do my taste buds!"

"Holy Grail Ale!" cried the priest, almost peeing himself with excitement. "Well, I suppose I could use a wee sip of the dark stuff!"

"Of course you could," said Dr. Delazny, smiling, raising his hand as though to give benediction. "There is treasure for you all. But remember. . . . the successful completion of this quest may well result in the saving of many lives, both human and Chinger!"

"Gee—that's great!" said Bgr. But he was the only one apparently who entertained that sentiment. The others had their attention too focused on their own personal gains to care much about the sparing of lives. As for Bill, his hormone and alcohol drenched brain vacillated between lust and booze. A steaming vision of his lost love merged with a full bottle until he couldn't tell the two apart. Which, basically, was fine with him. In his zonked-out state, it did not occur to him that what Dr. Delazny was asking him to do was to help pull the plug on his own lusts. But then, human desire has a way of muddling one's mind, causing one's puny rational abilities to shrivel up and blow away. For if, as the Ancients discovered, mediation places human consciousness in the Eternal Now, then surely lust places the body-mind web in the Eternal Rut. The notion of slaking his desires with Irma's agile help year after year, combined with a lifetime of Manure Technicianship, his own home on a quiet planet, all the alcohol he could drink, and *no more Troopers* was sufficient to short-circuit the perfidious chemo-behavioral wiring jury-rigged in his nervous system by the Empire, as well as to dampen the notion that this Quest might actually be fraught with horrendous dangers beyond his feeble imagination. Nor did he wonder if the game was worth the candle; he did not consider that Irma's beauty might fade with years. All of his attention, what little was left, was focused on the eternal *now*. The future would only be more of the same. Most certainly, he never considered that his already overtaxed liver might not be able to handle all the promised alcohol. But most especially, he hadn't the faintest idea that by this late stage of the game, his position in the Starship Troopers was as firmly wedded to his identity as the leather thong was to his neck, and his old Farmboy days were just as dead as the dove.

No, all these considerations were far beyond Trooper Bill's ken. His heart's desire was for Irma. Doctor Delazny had chosen well, for he had become, by this foggy stage, the archetypical Fool for Love.

So it was that when Dr. Delazny called this odd troop of travelers to attention, Bill obeyed without question.

"Right this way, folks," said the good Doctor, gesturing them to follow him. "The Aperture into the Paradigm lies in a room down the hall. We will toss your weapons in after you have stepped through the Portal. We don't want any accidents here, now do we?"

Bgr the Chinger, in his satyr outfit, herded them all toward the indicated room, chuckling enthusiastically and telling them how he intended to spend the peaceful years of his life, following the Armistice that would surely result after this excellent adventure. He would return to his studies, what intellectual joy. He described some of the repulsive alien races he had studied and thought of the slimy joys still untouched, and Bill cringed. Luckily, the lecture on exobiology ceased as they entered a large chamber, chock-a-block with computers and other extravagantly curved and angled machinery. Above it all, a gigantic Van der Graaf generator crackled fat zaps of electricity across its gap, frying the odd mosquito, moth or fly that escaped from the portal that yawned below it.

"Gulp!" sussurated Bill.

The other gulped as well. As well they might.

It was a round doorway, its edges rimmed with blinking red, green and cerulean lights. An occasional claw of energy would paw across the inlaid coppery metal work, or reach out and grab the air of the land beyond.

It was like peering through a window at a distant portion of landscape. It looked like a proscenium stage of a rococo production of a bad historical tragedy. Crumbling castles tilted in the distance, craggy mountains stuck out willy-nilly beyond. A blasted heath oozed ground fog, ridged with twisted, skeletal branches of trees, with gorse bushes and heather arrayed about simmering bogs like barbed wire about trenches. A chill wind sieved through the hole with faint hints of rotting vegetation and broad elbow-nudges of decomposing corpses.

Dr. Delazny grinned. "Bubble, bubble, toil and trouble, fellas! Now go find that Fountain of Hormones!"

From the Drunkards and Flagons came a collective gulp.

More gulps ensued as they knocked back large quantities of drink to embolden their flagging spirits.

One by one, they stepped through the portal. Bill's hair frizzed up, standing on end with the energy humming along the portal's periphery. Or was that the pure and simple terror that suddenly gripped his spine with ice-cold hands? His feet squelched into ankle deep muck. The smell grew truly horrendous; it was as though they had just stepped into some dragon's sulfurous lower bowels. When they were all through, Bgr and Dr. Delazny tossed their promised weapons after them.

Broadswords, daggers. Bows and arrows. Dirks and knives. Slingshots and Boy Scout knives.

"What the hell is this bowb?" cried out Rick the Supernal Hero, trying in vain to lift a broadsword out of the muck. "I need a blaster!"

"Afraid that modern technology doesn't work in this particular dimensional grid, Rick," Dr. Delazny shouted through the shrinking portal. "Bye bye now, folks. We'll be monitoring you!"

"Ixnay, ixnay!" said Rick, slogging forward. "This wasn't the deal!"

But before he could reach the portal, it clashed shut with a frizzle and a flash and Rick stumbled forward past where it had been, through misty air, tripped, and fell head first into a grayish green puddle.

Just then a horrendous, semi-human screech seared the atmosphere, like a skeleton's fingernails on a squeaky blackboard.

"I got idea," said Ottar, picking up the broadsword as though it were merely a particularly long toothpick and glowering about through his bushy eyebrows. "I going to like this place. What I kill first?"

CHAPTER 11

BILL CRAPS OUT

BILL LOOKED UP, SCREAMED HYSTERICAL-
ly, tried to run. There was no escape. The dragon's jaws
dropped down neatly over the head and body of Missionary Position, the Cattlelick priest. Teeth clamped
shut like a turbo-steam shovel, snapping off the priest's
legs at mid-calves. The elongated neck reared up—leaving priestly boots wobbling on the ground—the mouth
crunching and smacking.

Blood squirted out upon the party of adventures like
the jet of a sanguine lawn sprinkler just cutting on.

"Maybe the dragon won't be so hungry now," Rick
commented through chattering teeth, as the Supernal
Hero cowered behind Clitoria the Amazon.

"Better yet, maybe a bellyful of religion will poison

the monster!" sagely observed Hyperkinetic, who was
cowering behind Rick.

Bill, who in his precautionary, some would say cow-
ardly, turn was hiding behind Hyperkinetic, took the
remaining few guzzles of drink from his wineskin and
stared back at the creature, who was in the act of swal-
lowing his meal noisily and messily.

Bill had never seen a bigger dragon in his entire life.
This was a true and logical observation since, of course,
Bill had never seen a dragon before.

And this one was a particularly nasty-looking motherbowber. Gigantic bats' wings fanned out from its side,
their purplish, veiny membranes tattered at the edges,
shot through with holes here and there. Its body was a
scaly horror of reptilian revulsion, reddish green and
revolting, glistening and raw. From four long, well-
muscled limbs scythelike claws protruded, hung with
strips of the skins of its victims. But it was the thing's
head that was a particular abomination; bug eyes blood-
shot and rolling, nostrils scabrous and flaring, great
fangs depending from its hideous mouth, above which
a thick black mustache-like growth dangled.

In short it could be said that it looked like the dear
departed Deathwish Drang in one of his gentler, kinder
moments of recruit destruction.

"Beast!" cried Clitoria, her broadsword swishing
erect before the heinous monster. "Prepare to have thy
legs dismembered and jammed piece by bloody piece
down thy frightful, stenchy maw!"

"Javell!" cried Ottar, his own broadsword stabbed up
toward the low, rumbling clouds as though questing
for the power of the lightning. "And double from me,
too!"

The dragon raised its heavy, hairy eyebrows high on
its forehead. "Hey guys, have a care with those tooth-
picks," it said, reaching back and picking up its lit cigar
from the hole in the ground where the dragon had carefully placed it, then took a deep puff. "I'm a bleeder."

It tapped ash on Clitoria's blade. "Say you'all, did you know that I shot an elephant in my pajamas the other day. What it was doing in my pajamas, I'll never know."

It burped mightily and its smoky foul breath, redolent of disgusting items best left unmentioned, as well as alcoholic drink, and rump of priest, which can be mentioned, wafted down to the questers.

Bill realized that he should have seen this thing with the dragon coming. After all, the day's worth of trek across the hellish panorama of this dimensional plane had been unpleasantness piled upon misery, dismay stacked upon dismal disaster.

First, the questers had discovered that not only was the landscape fraught with odious smells, twisted sights and infernal noise, it also was populated by creatures who made the Chingers on Empire Propaganda posters look like dewy-eyed lambs. Fortunately, Clitoria and Ottar had a way with their broadswords and cut a nasty swath through the fiercely fanged teddy bears and the clawed giant plush animals—but it was only a matter of time before they stumbled across a mythical monster that was their match and more.

Second, it took only a few hours of slogging through the muddy swamps and nasty moors to discover that all of the staunch band of brothers, and one sister, uniformly loathed and detested one another. Even Rick and Bill—the best of buddies on board the starship named DESIRE—had words with each other, arguing about gagging, or possibly murdering, Hyperkinetic to eliminate his constant balladeering. It appeared that Rick actually enjoyed it and even joined in with a verse or two. Bill, though he'd loved Rick's ballad, found Hyperkinetic's songs ear-gratingly off-key and poorly rhymed—i.e. "bowb" and "duck"; "bowb" and "fit"; "bowb" and "mugger."

Thirdly, their liquor was rapidly running out, and they were all sobering up and realizing that agreeing to this journey across the twisted glandscape of the human psyche had been an incredible mistake of disastrous proportion.

A gigantic dragon squirming out of its cave and promptly chomping down on one of their members was the last thing their practically destroyed morale needed.

"Say the secret word and win a hundred dollars," said the dragon, confidently puffing away on its after-dinner cigar.

"Hack!" said Clitoria, waving her sword.

"Destroy!" roared Ottar, his own weapon windmilling above his head.

"Sorry. Neither of them correct. So how about you Three Morons standing over there with your jaws gaping adenoidally? Any takers?"

The barbaric duo, swords still awave, roared and were about to charge, but Rick, his eyes suddenly gleaming, a candle almost glimmering above his head (no lightbulbs here—no high technology) caught hold of his belt, dodged the outraged swipes of their swords, and whispered something in their ears. Grumbling, but nodding their heads, they lowered their weapons and stepped back a pace.

Maybe Rick's clever mind was going to get them out of this jam, thought Bill. He certainly hoped so.

Hyperkinetic plucked cacophonically upon his lute and lifted his head in song:

"The supernal Rick said, 'What the bowb.
Secret word? I'll try my luck!'"

"Would you be so kind as to please shut up," Bill suggested as he grabbed the man by his throat and throttled out an expiring gurgle.

"No, Bill, leave him be," said Rick, prying Bill's fingers loose. "He may be off-key—but he's quite right." Rick the Supernal Hero swung around to face the leering, cigar-smoking dragon. "Well then dragon. Arrr! The secret word, then. But if we say this secret word, will you let us pass unmolested?"

"Sound fair to me. I've had my dinner." The dragon rubbed his protuberant tummy happily and belched another cloud of smoke.

"All right then, but dragon—there must be all of several hundred words in your vocabulary! Low odds on picking the right one!"

"Please!" huffed the dragon. "I know one hundred and thirty-three thousand words at least—and that just in English!" He burped. "That, for an example, was an 'eructation.'"

"Sounds like an old fashioned belch to me," mumbled Bill. His nerves were getting frayed. And, more important, he was becoming uncomfortably sober.

"Marvelous," Rick marveled. "Which means that the odds on my choosing the secret one are truly astronomical." Rick paced back and forth, pursing his lips and clearly thinking very hard. Suddenly, his finger smote the air and he spun to face the dragon. "I know. Surely a dragon of your clear intelligence and erudition can construct a riddle around this secret word. . . . So that we might have some slim chance of getting it right!"

"Hmmm!" said the dragon. "And why not. I like riddles, though it's my good buddy Winks the Sphinx who uses them the most. But blast it, whatever Winks can do, *I* can do as well. You'll have to give me a few minutes to think one up, though. And you'll have to realize that if you don't get it right, you have to lay down your weapons and allow me to eat you all, one by one."

"Certainly, certainly," said Rick, allowing the others to see the crossed fingers he had put behind his back. "But good dragon. A few preliminary questions. What, pray tell, is your name?"

"My name? Why, Smog, of course. Yes, I'm called Smog, because of certain habits I have." He pointed at the lit cigar and grinned.

"And what land are we presently traveling through?"

"Land? You do not know the name of this *land*?" The dragon snarfed with amusement. "Why, it is the Country of Absurd Fantasy of course. It is the subconscious territory of the human mind whence writers of imagination fill their ink wells to assay splendid novels of High Comedy! It is the part of the Over-Gland where puns are the highest form of humor, and juxtaposition of the mundane and myth produce hearty chuckles in flocks and flocks of faithful readers!" The dragon peeled off his eyebrows and mustache. "Hence the Groucho Marx imitation. Pretty funny, huh?"

Rick managed a laugh, but Bill, who had never heard of Groucho Marx, could only slap on an unconvincing goofy grin.

"Yes, yes. Very funny, Smog. One more question, and then you can have a moment to think up your riddle. Have you heard of a place called the Fountain of Hormones!"

"The Fountain of Hormones! Why yes! *Everybody's* has heard of the Fountain of Hormones! It's in the very center of this terrain, right between the Land of Feelthy Magazines, and Bodiceripper Romances." The dragon lifted a claw and pointed. "You go south all the way." It grinned and licked its lips. "That is you go south *if* you answer my riddle correctly." Smog scratched his ear with one great filthy claw, making an irritating rasping sound, then reared up to its full height and gazed down with fascination at its pronounced belly-button. "Come to think of it, folks, you go south *either* way!"

Clitoria and Ottar rattled their swords and snarled, but Rick silenced them with a gesture.

"We'll give you a few minutes of silence to concoct your riddle. Meantime, we will just step a short distance around yonder hill, where we may tinkle in the bushes. You don't want to gobble down travelers full of it, do you?"

Superb, thought Bill. What a great thinker Rick was! All they'd have to do when they got past that hill was to take off for the South. There was no way that those flimsy, tatty wings of Smog were going to keep him aloft to follow very long.

"No way, Sonny," the dragon said, though. "I've heard that old bowb before. Once around the hill and you are in the next county in seconds. Besides, I've got my riddle. Are you ready? I'm only going to give you to the count of ten to answer, folks, and then I'm going to gobble you up!" He winked at them. "Oh, this is a really good one! Are you ready for it?!" The dragon snickered coyly. Which, when you think about it, is a pretty repelling sight.

"Riddle on, Smog!" said Rick, standing up to every inch of his heroic height.

"Very well, tender people. The riddle:

"What travels on four legs at dawn, two legs at midday, and three at dusk?"

The dragon leered at them, waggling his eyebrows knowingly. Rick slapped his forehead. "Gosh. Arrrrr! That's a hard one. You'll excuse us while my friends and I huddle together on the matter."

"Of course," said the dragon. "But the count begins now," it reminded them. "One!" it rumbled.

The group convened, frowns of puzzlement all around. For Bill's part, he didn't have the faintest. It was the stupidest riddle he'd ever heard!

"I know!" ventured Hyperkinetic, tapping his long narrow nose. "A Martian orgy! At least, that's the answer I thought I saw in GALACTIC PLAYBOY Party Jokes!"

Rick shook his head. "We're not in the land of Feelthy Magazines yet! We're in the land of Absurd Fantasy. We need something appropriate."

"Two!" growled Smog.

"Chingers?" ventured Bill hopelessly and they all looked at him with disgust.

"Three!" drooled Smog.

"Let us not be *too* stupid, Bill." said Rick. "I know

a lot of morons that would have a hard job coming up with something that dumb."

"Tempers, tempers, time's a-wasting. Four!" cozened Smog.

"I know what is!" said Ottar happily. "Sammy Wallund, come home after all-night drink, stagger, fall on face . . ."

"Five!" roared Smog.

"No, no, no!" said Rick, beginning to tear at his hair. "I know it! It's on the tip of my tongue, but I just can't spit it out!"

"Six!" sneered Smog.

"How about a Denubian Slime Dog?" ventured Clitoria.

"What comes after six?" asked Smog, starting to count on his claws. "Oh yes! Eight!" But the bewildered dragon was running out of said-bookisms, so he just declared this number in a simple monotone.

"Man," said Bill. "This is one *tough* riddle!"

"Seven!"

"That's it!" cried Rick. "That's the answer!" He scampered over to the dragon, waving his arms wildly. "Ed Rex told me this one in the Holy Bar and Grill!"

"Ten!" said Smog. "You guys come up with the answer or what?"

"Yes, I think so," said Rick. "What walks on four legs in the morning, two in midday and three at dusk, Smog? Why, a *man* of course! Four legs when he crawls after he's born, two when he is a mature man—and then three, in the twilight of his years, 'cause he needs a *cane!* Where'd you get that one, fellow? Your sphinxy buddy, Winks?"

Smog's lips curled unhappily. "Drat. I should have dug a little deeper in my riddle memory. Oh well. That's the way the corpses crumple."

"Then we get to leave now?" Bill cried happily. "Can you also maybe let us know where the nearest bar is?"

"No to the first question—and I don't know to the

second," the dragon sussurated succinctly through a singularly wicked grin. "I have no intention of letting such
succulent suckers as yourselves go! Besides, I've rather
a hankering for a good, long bloody fight!"

No sooner were the words spoken, than its great head
speared forward, planting its considerable fangs around
Hyperkinetic and his lute. The bard was quickly drawn
up into the air, wriggling and screaming most unmusi-
cally, and then swallowed down with a gigantic gulp,
following the priest to digestive destiny.

"Lying lout!" cried Clitoria, raising her sword for
battle.

"You lie to Ottar!" bellowed the Viking, sword whistling in fast circles. "Ottar chop you into *hundemad*, dog
food!"

"Well, at least no more bad ballads!" Bill philoso-
phized, dragging out his sword. Since the Troopers used
only guns and heavy weapons, he wasn't sure how well
he could handle one of these. He could only hope that
his instincts and great desire for survival might teach
him quickly enough.

Rick's weapons were also drawn. "Go get the foul
fiend!" he cried. "I'll guard the rear!"

The barbarians trundled forward, slashing, feinting
and stabbing at the green, snarling beast.

"That's a good idea," Bill agreed as a roaring blast of
flame wrapped him in soot. He saw the flashing claws
of the dragon rake out toward the barbarians. "We never
can be sure who's going to attack from our backs, can
we?"

Clitoria and Ottar were oblivious. They had turned
into the fierce, fighting-machine berserkers that were
their nature. Swinging their broadswords, they dived
happily into battle.

Unfortunately, the battle was over much too swiftly
for Bill's taste.

Ottar was swiftly gutted and then swallowed down

in three or four chunks, whiskey bottles in his pockets and all.

Clitoria was slightly more successful. She managed to scratch the dragon here and there, but as soon as Smog's gullet was free of Ottar, he snatched the woman up and sent her right after him.

Using the sword as a toothpick, Smog turned and smiled down at the two remaining travelers, leering sanguinely through the blood smeared on his chops.

"Yum, yum! And now, for dessert. Who goes first? The clever one or the stupid one!"

"Him!" cried Rick, pointing at Bill.

"No, him!" cried Bill, pointing at Rick.

"My, my, what a frightful choice." The dragon pounded forward toward them, bent over them, leering obscenely, its stomach a bloated green wall of flesh, the belly button as big as a pool table popping out at them. Bill blinked up, shivering with fear, blinked again at the dragonian umbilicus, at the brass head of a screw in the middle of it. A screw?

For want of anything better to do, faced with certain death in any case, he jabbed the point of his sword into the slot in the screwhead. And turned.

"Don't *do* that!" the dragon screamed in a high girlish falsetto. Then shrieked again, weaker and feebler. The next scream was hard to hear at all.

And began to fade away.

But as the dragon grew dimmer ghastly shapes appeared in its stead. Dark forms that coalesced and shimmered.

Something pretty exotic was taking place.

AN EXTRA,
FREE BONUS!

NORMALLY A SERIOUS WORK OF FUTURE history, such as this volume that you are holding in your trembling hands, would be empty of illustrations. This despicable business has now changed. You can *see* the future! This has come about through an exclusive contract signed with the Schlochmeister Sex Foundation. For the first time a photographic record has been made of the operation of the subconscious brain, the Over-Gland and that kind of thing. Most of these pix were pretty repulsive—one editor died after looking at them!—so you will be seeing only the approved ones.

But they are still pretty raunchy. So we advise that if you are under sixteen, or over fifteen, that you skip these pix—avert your eyes!—and skip right ahead to the next page of text.

REMEMBER—YOU WERE WARNED!

Bill, yet again, is having foot trouble. Not wildly enthusiastic about the new one, is he!

No, he is kissing Irma's hand, not eating it! What a sordid mind you have... Almost as bad as that of the peeping-tom satyr in the background.

Holding a dead dove isn't easy when you have two right hands and no opposable thumbs. Bill has yet to realize the dead dove makes him a dead duck.

Captain Rick, not the most graceful of jerks, manages
to almost fall himself dead.

Bill, ever the resourceful Trooper, craftily slips in a quick thirty winks while Rick and Archmedes try to BS each other to death.

The bartender at the Bar and Grill makes a pig of himself . . .

A graphic example of the evil affects of drink—followed
by . . .

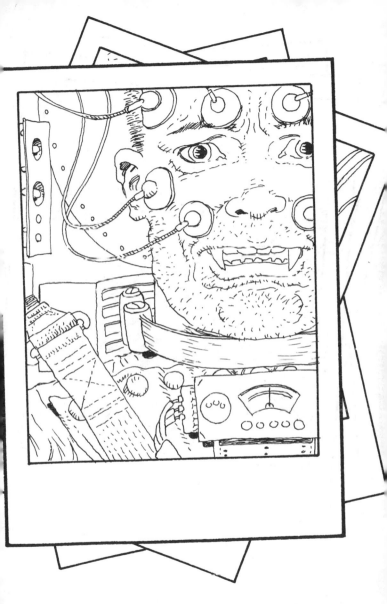

... the same repellent scene as seen by Dr. Delazny.

The halitosis kid in action—dragon's breath in noisome close-up.

The moving finger points; Captain Rick, for reasons best known to himself, indicates a particularly flat-looking castle.

Bill in deep yogurt. Chained and surrounded by a grotesque collection of trolls and troglodytes—not to mention the unwelcome attentions of the Barren Baron.

If you've seen one bio-computer, you've seen them all.
Bill is suitably impressed.

Bill is not the only one. A sub-editor went out the window of the thirtieth floor when he saw this pic. Be strong and hurriedly turn the page—or you could be the next!

This is better. A jazzy pic of Pecos Bill gazing smarmily at his Chinger pardner.

Until you have seen a six-armed, six-inch tall, six-gun-shooting alien lizard you have seen nothing. Send this one to the Guinness Book of Records.

CHAPTER 12

ALONE AND
LIMPLY LOITERING

"WELL FOR THE LOVE OF BEELZEBUBBA!"
said Rick, frozen with astonishment at the sight, just as
Bill was. "Will you take a look at that!"

As the dissolving dragon grew ever mistier dark forms
began to coalesce in the area, approximately where the
creature's stomach must have been. Streamers of ecto-
plasmic mist billowed up coating the mysterious shapes
in feathery cocoons. Within this thick, localized fog fizzled and glinted majestic sparklers of energy, like
Pseudo-Fourth of July on Mistworld in the Pleiades Sector.

"Wow," Rick observed. "This sure beats late night
holovision." Then fear hit. "I'm not sure I like this.
What's happening?"

"It could be anything, worry-wart. But that carnivorous dragon *was* dangerous and it's well vanished. Just keep your sword handy and we'll see what gives now."

Some sort of transformation, it would seem. . . .

Bill leaned closer and watched. Within the glowing bulbs of fog, he thought he saw the reweaving of flesh, the rejoining of connective tissue. But before he could do much more thinking on the subject, one of the thrumming bulbs broke open with a gaseous sigh.

Stepping out, like a new-hatched chick from its egg-shell, came a gangling adolescent, blinking through concave horn-rimmed glasses the size of radiation visors. The young man was afflicted with acne and had a cold sore on his lip. The top button of his flannel shirt was buttoned, and his belted pants were fastened almost up to the base of his rib cage. In his top shirt pocket, pens and pencils peeked out from a plastic pocket protector.

"Hi! I'm Peter Perkins!" he announced perspicaciously. "Looks like I got wasted, huh? Oh well, I was getting kind of bored with the Priest character anyway." He looked down at his palm, in which he held a number of multi-sided dice. "Maybe I'll wander on up the street and see what's cooking at the game at Weird Alfred's." He looked with distaste at the surroundings, then at Rick and Bill. "He's a better Game Master, anyway. What do you say, guys?"

The "guys" were the others rising up from their misty bulbs, steaming with their foggy afterbirth. They were uniform only in their adolescence and bad complexions, the dice cupped in their hands, and general nerdiness. One was a grossly fat boy, munching on a Lactic Way candy bar. Another was a short, ugly boy wearing a ratty Boy Scout outfit. The last was female, in a kind of generally bloated manner, with a man-hating sneer on her pasty, pudgy face.

Bill scratched his head. "What the bowb's going on here, guys?"

"Don't you see, Bill?" said Rick, a glow of understanding washing over his face like an incoming tide of comprehension. "Dr. Delazny and the Chinger structured this as a role-playing game! These are just gamers from some other dimension, world or such that they picked up."

"Yeah, and he's a really *lousy* Game Master too," whined the girl, presumably formerly Clitoria.

"You bet," said the formerly-Ottar fellow. "A homophagous dragon with lousy riddles. The Fountain of Hormones—an equally disastrous idea. The land of Absurd Fantasy?" He stared over at the two bemused soldiers of fortune and blinked at them. "Rick the Supernal Hero? Yeah, and this joker is really supposed to be Bill— as in Bill, the Galactic Hero! Right! And I'm Jason dinAlt of Deathworld!" The teenager snorted in contempt. "Let's blow this popsicle stand, guys, and get into a game with some *hair* on its chest."

"Yeah!" said the last, peering about him in a bored manner. "Where are the dwarves with the great big axes? And I bet these jokers haven't even read their Hickman and Weis!"

The others looked horrified at the very thought.

"Wait a minute," said Rick, scratching his head with apparent bafflement. "I thought this scenario was supposed to be the Over-Gland fantasy segment, based upon archetypes, myths, fairy tales and suchlike hundreds, even thousands of years old."

"Myths? Fairy tales? What are those? This is serious gaming, man!" announced the militant fantasy gamer female. "This is *important stuff!*"

"Yeah!" said the others in unison. "This place stinks!"

With that, they started shaking their hands, and their dice rattled and clicked. Motion lines jerked and swayed about them, courtesy of some unseen cartoonist perhaps, and with one final spectacular swirl of animated mist, they started to spin and spin and spin . . . .

Into nothingness.

"Wow!" said Bill. "They disappeared. Just like that.

Say, Rick. Think we can do that? I don't really like this place much either."

"No, Bill." Rick sighed. "I'm afraid we've been real patsies. We've been had by that Doctor and that Chinger. We're in this for the duration. The only way we're going to get out of this is to find that Fountain of Hormones for them."

"That bowbing Eager Chinger Bgr," gurgled Bill, his urgent need for Irma lessening somewhat, replaced by a sudden need for pure and simple revenge. "I'll get even with him for doing this to me."

"And don't forget Delazny!" grumbled Rick.

"No. I won't forget Doctor Delazny. I've got something very special planned for him!" Bill's eyes glimmered with hatred and calculation. "Keelhauling Doctor Latex Delazny in deep space is too good for him!"

Rick agreed, and they continued on their journey southwards, away from the land of Absurd Fantasy and toward the doubtlessly much more worthwhile and interesting Land of Feelthy Magazines.

Unfortunately, they had no compass.

Which meant that with very little effort on their part they managed to get themselves terribly lost. Bill, who had been looking forward with tumescent expectation to squadrons of frolicking nudes, badly written yet graphic lascivious prose, as well as not funny cartoons with incredibly endowed lovelies in compromising situations, was disappointed to find himself in a new and depressing territory filled with almost unrelieved gloom.

"Arrrr!" observed Rick, looking about him at the wilted vegetation, the monochrome colors. There was an entire lack of any kind of smell to the air, be it foul or fair. The limbs of what few trees there were about drooped listlessly. The grass and the weeds lay pasted down upon the ground damply, as though they'd just been pelted by a fierce, not to say slimy, storm. Indeed, the entire glandscape had the appearance of nothing less than *limpness* as though all hint of life or vitality had been bled from every object.

"Zoroaster!" growled Bill. "Looks like this place has a terminal vitamin deficiency!"

"Grim, eh? Arrrr! I think we've traveled a bit off course, matey, and even now find ourselves upon the Fabled Isthmus of Impotence."

Bill cringed, filled with instant fear. The very term was anathema to an alcohol-blooded Trooper of the Empire, striking terror deep with the much-cherished macho self-image that was the eternal legacy of male-dominated society. Or something like that. And he wasn't worried about "Fabled" or "Isthmus." It was that terrible "I" word that got him.

"But this is supposed to be the all-powerful Over-Gland, fueled by the powerful chemical reactions of the collective overactive Ids of billions of human beings!" Bill suggested.

Rick shrugged. "Maybe it had a tough day at the office."

"No. It must be something more than that. I've got the feeling, in fact, that it's something very important." He scanned the stale, flat, underwhelming territory. "We have got to figure this out. Do you have any idea of what is happening?"

"In a word—no."

"*But you know, Bill,*" Bill said in a strange and hollow voice. "I didn't say that," he said, clapping his hands over his mouth.

"I heard you say it," Rick cannily observed.

"*This is your friend, the good Dr. Delazny,*" Bill said again in the same strange voice. "*Speaking to you through the benefit of post-hypnotic impression. If you are hearing this now it is because you find yourself in a situation that your teeny-tiny brains cannot understand or explain. Therefore I, or at least my voice, is here to help. That you have activated this particular pseudo-memory means that you are now dis-*

covering something new about human beings. Common knowledge to the medical profession, but shocking news to you dummies that even within the young overexcited stud, there is still some part that the surging hormones do not affect. This must be the symbolic part that I have mentioned to you before, though you probably weren't listening—the neo-cortex. The source of logic and reason in mankind."

"Naw," said Rick. "This place is much too big for that."

Bill spoke again in his new voice, muffled a bit since he had both hands over his mouth. "*You jokers will have to figure this out for yourselves since I am really not there. Perhaps you have reached the Fountain of Hormones that you were supposed to find. Get to work. Over and out.*"

Rick scratched his chin. He surveyed the territory again. "What about that castle over there, Bill?"

"What castle?" he said in his usual gravelly voice. Then yipped with pleasure. "It's gone! It's me talking again!"

"Wonderful. I liked the other voice better. It had something to say. Now we're on our own again. Over there, see it? On the hill. The clouds are just lifting even as I speak."

Sure enough, as Bill looked to the spot that Rick had indicated, he saw the cottony sheath of gray clouds lifting like a curtain on the next section of a play, revealing the battlements of a particularly flat-looking castle with stubby towers and a droopy flag dangling from a droopy mast.

"Surely we can knock on that castle's doors and ask for directions!" Rick suggested, his spirits plainly rising.

After a quick, if soggy trek, they found themselves standing before the portcullis of the castle.

"Yoo-hoo!" called Rick. "Is anyone home? We are but weary, hungry and thirsty travelers searching for a warm fire, a cold drink of—water, maybe a hot meal and simple directions!"

A door opened behind the guardian bars of the portcullis. A nose peeked out. "Who's there!" whined a nasal voice, reminiscent of a chipmunk with a bad head cold.

"Rick and Bill!" said the Supernal Hero in the friendliest, most diplomatic voice he could manage.

"Rick and Bill aren't here!"

The door slammed shut. Bill pounded on the metal-studded wood slats of the portcullis. "Hey, bowbhead. *We're* Rick and Bill! We need some help!"

"Please, Bill," hissed Rick. "We need to be a little friendlier if we want to get anywhere. We're not exactly in a Trooper barracks, you know."

Thank Zoroaster for that, thought Bill, who had taken to wearing body armor to bed after that spate of D.I. murders by recruits in the Beta Dacroni Sector. Officials claimed it was the effect of Zeta-wave radiation from the primary that had driven the killers out of their teeny-tinys—but Bill knew the truth. After all, *he'd* been a recruit once, under the heel of the much-loathed, always-feared, Deathwish Drang. One of his dearest dreams during those months of grueling torture, a dream undoubtedly shared by everyone else in the barracks, had been to preside over the torture and eventual execution of Drang.

The door creaked open and the nose peered out again. "Oh! *You're* Rick and Bill. And ye say you want directions? Well, heh-heh, you go to hell—and I'll tell you how to find that!"

"Actually," cried Rick, desperately, "we're salesmen! Right! And we're selling Grandma Goldfarb's Old Fashioned Monkey-Liver Hair Restorer, along with a special offer, today only, on Grandpa Goldfarb's Guardia Gorilla-Gland Potency Serum! Think about that—have you ever seen an undersexed gorilla? The answer, of course, is no. And it—it—" said Rick, running out of inspiration.

The door squeaked back open tentatively, and the nose stuck out again. "Don't need hair restorer much," it wheezed (and Bill could see from the tangled growths of hair coming from the nostrils that this statement was quite true). "But there has been a slight problem around here lately that the latter potion might resolve." A moment of silence; Bill could almost hear the rusty gears grinding. "Very well, strangers. Put down your weapons, and I'll take you in for an audience with the master."

Gladly, Bill and Rick removed their swords and daggers and threw them on the ground. The door of the castle swung open all the way, and a narrow man in a shapeless hat from which a tangle of limp hair hung down to his shoulders leaned out. Seeing that they were disarmed he hit a lever, and with a cranking wheeze and a rattle of chains the portcullis slowly clanked up. "Walk this way," he said through a protuberant nose, his small badger eyes gesturing them to follow. The tall thin man spun round and stumbled rapidly away, clicking his heels against the stone floor with every step.

Bill and Rick attempted the strange loping shuffle and click, but to little effect. By the time they'd reached the courtyard of the castle, they'd given up entirely.

"Did you read that sign?" asked Rick.

"Sign?" said Bill. "What sign? I'm was too busy trying to walk this ridiculous walk."

"Maybe it's significant. I better just run back and take a look."

Bill continued on after the strange-looking man, stepping out into the gray daylight of the courtyard. The first thing that he was aware of was that the man who'd let them in had disappeared. The second was the dozens of unsheathed swords and arrowheads pointed toward his most vulnerable body. Connected to said weapons was a collection of the ugliest creatures Bill had ever seen in his life, and Bill had seen some very ugly things, especially after a good drunk and looking into the mirror. Orcs and trolls crouched and slobbered, brandishing pointed weapons. Gnomes and dwarves raised axes and knives.

"Here we go, Bill!" said Rick from back in the passageway. "It's a bit dim back here, but I think I can read it. Says, 'Abandon . . . Hope. . . . All. . . . Ye. . . . Who. . . . Enter. . . . Here.' Now what do you suppose they mean by that, Bill?"

Bill didn't answer. He was too busy spinning about in a circle, looking for a way out.

Unhappily, with very little success.

CHAPTER 13

IN LOW DUNGEON

THE DUNGEON WAS THE PITS. CERTAINLY not the most pleasant place in the universe, though there was a good possibility that it was fighting for bottom place as the worst. To help alleviate his black depression Bill tried to find a good side to look upon. It took some time. He finally came up with the feeble argument that, basically, perhaps he had to admit it was better than boot camp. The swill they fed him was superior, mixed up with the occasional cockroach for protein. In fact, since the mixture had apparently been left lying around for weeks after preparation, underneath the mold he scratched off, it tended to be fermented, which left Bill with a most satisfactory buzz. Though it didn't exactly make him drunk since he was only presented with this

repulsive feast at intervals, at least he didn't have to stay
sober all of the time.

Cruel fate! Would he never have a chance to see his
cherished Irma again?

Bill despaired of the very hope of it, muttering and
moaning damp-eyedly to himself in self-pity. It was
very cathartic.

The one thing that irked him the most here though,
were the chains. There were rings around his neck, his
wrists and his arms, and these were connected to thick,
heavy chains that were in turn connected to the wall.
When he was sleeping or when he was just sitting, they
weren't too bad, but they made moving around very
difficult. Since it wasn't likely that he'd be able to get
through the non-existent windows, or the narrow bars,
he didn't see the purpose of the chains, so they were
particularly annoying. He complained about them every
time the hunchback came to feed him and change his
slop-bucket, but since the bent little dwarf seemed to
be deaf, as well as simple, it did little good.

Too bad about that business in the courtyard.

By hindsight, 20–20 hindsight, it looked like it really
hadn't been such a great idea to come to this particular
castle after all. It had seemed such a harmless enough
castle, and who could have predicted the army of creatures awaiting them in the courtyard. If only they hadn't
come up with that Gorilla-Gland business—then the
shambling servant wouldn't have let them in, and they
wouldn't have had to try and prove its efficacy, with
dozens of weapons trained on them. Naturally, since it
did not exist, Rick had the really wonderful idea of
pretending that his flask full of wine was the special
medicine they were hawking. "To be rubbed on lo-
cally," he'd explained. "Arrrrrr! As a matter of fact, this
is a sample. Why don't you just keep it and use it at
your leisure. Meanwhile, my companion and I must
push off and be about our business."

Unfortunately, the assembled bestiary had insisted

upon a demonstration of the efficacy of the medicine then and there, stripping their captives of their trousers and then splashing the "Gorilla-Gland" fluid on the appropriate parts.

Predictably, the results were less than impressive. If anything, the chilled wine had the reverse, shrinking effect. The muttering grew in volume, nor were they at all convinced when Rick shouted out that it sometimes took a while to take effect.

Alas, not one troll, not one dwarf, nor even an orc, bought this line. The duo were dutifully marched off to separate dungeons without even the dignity of the return of their trousers.

So here was Bill, rotting away in the dark. He'd no idea at all how many days had passed, since there was no difference here in the smelly hay-strewn cell between day and night. There was just the occasional serving of fermented swill to mark the crawling passage of time.

Oh well, thought Bill. This wasn't exactly the Vulcanian Riviera, but at least he could loaf around all day on his back and get some much-needed rest. For as long as he could remember, his life had been just go-go-go! If there wasn't a group of raw recruits to train and mutilate, it was some hare-brained emergency to deal with. Besides, here he could actually do something that he hadn't done much in years and years.

Sleep.

Ever since that recruiter had come stumping along with that one-robot band and signed him up for the service, Bill had forgotten how very much he truly enjoyed a good bit of the good old sack time.

Now, without electronic reveille electrically juicing up every fiber of his being, not to mention his body, at some repulsive early hour of the morning, he found that he could drift in the restful pools of somnolence for delirious long stretches, and so for awhile he did just that, putting paid to his sleep debt. But when Bill got his fill of sleeping, it really did get boring after awhile;

he realized that there really wasn't much else to do down here!

Fortunately, after the first day or two (three? five? twenty?) of mildly alcohol-numbed tedium, Bill remembered that he'd brought along a book. Or rather, *many* books, come to think of it! Yes! For still there in his sinus cavity was the BLEEDERS'S DIGEST he had so fortuitously lifted from the Terminal Ward at the Hospital on Colostomy IV.

And one of the books, it turned out, was a very large shared-universe theme collection entitled HERETICS IN HADES. As Bill had thoroughly enjoyed a previous shared-universe anthology he'd read entitled DEBTOR'S WORLD, he dove into the spine-connected read-out with great glee:

HERETICS IN HADES
"Gilganosh Meets Two Pulp Fiction Writers"
by
Robot Goldilocks
"War is Hell"
Popular military expression.

If Gilganosh was truly born with the dead lo! so many centuries ago, then now he truly was *bored* of the dead.

With his mighty thewed limbs he ran ahunting amongst the wild Outhouses, wantonly skewering hell-beasties with his bow and his sharp arrows, conversing with famous Caesars of Rome and Kings of Africa and other dead folk condemned to the perditious gray lands of Hades, and flexing his biceps for the New Tourists and their new-fangled electronic Nikons and Leicas, their Sony videocams. See how the Great King of Uruk prances about half-naked for these strange people in their Bermuda shorts and their Hawaiian shirts and their dark sunglasses. Oh mighty

King of cities that are now dust! Oh hairy, wild King! Thy head is as a lion's with a glorious mane; thy feet are like the tanks of the neo-Nazi who would defeat the mighty Pluto himself; thy droppings are as great as logs.

Socrates! Plato! Augustus Caesar! Agamemnon! Sumeria! Babylonia! Greece! Now that the historical name-dropping fit is quit from these rapid keyboarding fingers to show off the erudition and sophistication of yours truly, I, the author, Robot Goldilocks, not wasting a drop of research from my historical novel, I, GILGANOSH, nor from one of my early non-fictional efforts, A GUIDE TO EARLY SOFT-CORE PORN MYTHS, I shall plunge forward on the tides of my beautiful, facile prose and segue most expertly (like a ballerina pirouetting to Tchaikovsky's *Swan Lake*? Like Joseph Conrad, or Philip Roth or, better yet, those fabulous writers of yore, Henry Kuttner and C.L. Moore!) into just why Gilganosh was bored.

Oh Gilganosh! Oh mighty hero of millennia past! You're bored, you putz, because you have been alive for century after century, here in Hades where you can't really die! You're bored because you miss your good buddy, Inky-Dinky-Doo, with whom you've had a quarrel and who promises to hack off and serve you up your barrelwide backside on a platter if you ever cross chariots again!

However, harken! A great adventure lies just around the corner! Coming down that hill yonder! Is that a great mythological beast pawing and snorting up dust as it spumes across the wilderness?

No! Why, the thing is as anachronistic as the digital Mickey Mouse watch upon thy mighty wrist!

Lo! It's a Ford Bronco four by four!

The mighty vehicle roared along through the bush of the Hades Outhouse territory, while the driver and his

passenger argued amicably, chewing over a favorite old
subject, like Cthulhu chews his cud.

"Lordy, H.P.!" drawled the beefy, red faced one,
sweating and grinning as he kept the wheel of the truck
under control. "I don't think there's a shee-eet of a lot
of a contest! I was a hell of a lot weirder than you were!"

"Were not!"

"Was too!"

They were speaking, of course, these dead fantasists,
of their days on Earth before they had died and gone to
Hades, that great mythical hole in the ground curiously
mutated now as though by some techno-thriller writer's
imagination on downers, coupled perhaps with some
warped Latin teacher's lust for Roman history (there was
a curious preponderance of the Roman Empire hereabouts, it seemed). They were talking about the halcyon
days of yore, the nineteen twenties and the thirties, when
both strode like collosi through the pulpy pages of
ARGOSY, INSCRUTABLE ORIENTAL SPICY
YARNS and, of course, that paragon of the tale of the
outré, WEIRD TALES. Both had died in 1936, Howard
of a self-inflicted gunshot wound to his head upon learn-
ing that his beloved Ma was dying; Lovecraft of cancer
of the esophagus, almost surely brought about by his
curious diet, and perhaps the secret indulgence in certain
fungi. Yes, yes, stable characters indeed, both of them;
their one-way trips to Hades had done them both a load
of good. Howard had his Ma around now forever; Lovecraft a feast of history, the outré—and fungi, and the
total certainty that behind all this strange business were
none other but the Old Ones themselves!

Living myths in a land of mythic living! Ah! Sic transit
gloria mundi, Tuesday, or something like that.

"Shee—eet, H.P. Ah'm from Texas," proclaimed
Bob Howard proudly. "We just grow everything bigger
there, and my weird's bigger than yours! Did you pound
out reams and reams of oriental mysteries, westerns,
spicy romances, supernatural monster stories and fi-

nally, did you help invent that pin-ay-cull of literature, sword and sorcery, featuring a hero swiped directly from Rousseau and Burroughs, the classic character Conan?" He paused for a deep breath. "Did you off yourself at the age of thirty after years of espousing the heroic life in penny-a-word pulp rags because you couldn't live without Mommy? Did you drool over bare-chested goddesses and amazons in your thumping, pumping prose when you didn't have the nerve to go out and lose your cherry to a two-dollah whore in Houston?" Howard shook his corpulent head, a lop-sided grin on his wide face. "Now, H.P., we corresponded lots back in those days. Now, I admit, mebbe your stories were a mite weirder than mine at times—but deep down, I'm in a different class of weird. Big weird. Texas weirdo. Living weird! Dead now, of course, but weird dead is *weird*. There ain't nothin' more way out than that!"

Howard Phillips Lovecraft shook his head with etiolated pity.

"Ah, my poor Robert E.! Tsk and tsk again. You died much too young to have the *opportunity* to truly perfect the subtle points of weirdness, as I did. I realize, Robert, that you were basically a racist, but that was purely cultural, a product of your backward pigsty Texan environment. My racism was truly a moldy bacterial culture, tended and pruned carefully in my decaying Providence basement! You were very fuzzy headed about your Aryan sympathies, Bob. I openly proclaimed the superiority of the white race. In fact, I'm sure you are aware that much of my actual paltry income was earned as a ghost writer. But did you realize that in the twenties, I had a student in a correspondence course for the Famous Bigot Writer's School who paid me to ghost a book called MEIN KAMPF? Yes, as a matter of fact, I met the fellow back in New Berlin a few months ago down here. As soon as he finishes his present thirteen millennia neck deep in sulfuric acid, while suffering terminal athlete's foot, and before he starts a thousand year swim in the main cesspit, he wants to get in some fast outlining. Looks as though he's in the market for another book!

"Anyway, did you live on cornflakes and milk half your life? Did you create possibly the sickest fictional mythology known to man? Did you live in a rotting old house in a particularly diseased state, slowly festering away on the putrid fumes of illness, cranking out loony letters to fellow pulp writers when you should have been doing some honest penny-a-word westerns? Like you, Bob, who made more money than your local doctor. Now, admit it, Bob. You were most definitely weird, but I, my friend, to put it in one syllable words that even a Texan can understand, I was not only *much* weirder—I was the fruitcake of the century!"

Their argument was suddenly cut short as the four by four plowed into the solid form standing staunch and unafraid before it.

The Bronco stopped dead.

When H.P. and Robert E. recovered, they found themselves staring up into the frowning face of the biggest man that either of them had ever seen.

"Hey, slimeball," roared Gilganosh affectionately, tearing off a fender angrily. "Don't you watch where you're going?"

Gilganosh was dying inside.

Oh, not because he had just been hit by a four by four of the automotive persuasion; there were far greater thorns in his side, routine passengers of life. Bemusedly he plucked out some of the thorns and discarded them. No, it was because he grieved at the anger that his greatest friend, Inky-Dinky-Do held for him. He felt worse than Shadrach in the furnace must have felt; no starry ascent to the heavens for Great Gilganosh; it was all purely downward to the Earth for this Son of Man, borne on failing nightwings, perhaps to be impaled on some awful tower of glass below.

Gilganosh looked upon the two occupants of the Bronco with distaste. "You've got the whole wide open plains of the Outhouse to roam in, and you pinheads manage to drive with your eyes shut and hit *me*."

The soft, fat, largish man with a crew-cut and a ruddy complexion managed to struggle out from his seat behind the wheel, to waddle corpulently forward. "Jumpin' Jehosophatical jack rabbits! It's Conan!" he hollered. "Conan of Cimmeria, I swear, right down to the corpuscles!"

Gilganosh blinked, bewildered. What nonsense was this New-Corpse mouthing? He'd met a Conan once, but that fellow was the character who believed in fairies and wrote those Sherlock Holmes and Professor Challenger stories.

"Now Bob, settle down," said the lardy one's companion, a tall, pale looking New-Corpse with pasted back hair, fishy eyes and a lantern jaw. "Conan is just a fantasy, a concoction of your stylistically incompetent keyboard."

Bob nodded. "Sure, I know that, H.P. But cut me some slack. I always was a closet nancy-boy, and now I've got a chance to *make* it with the biggest, hairiest, most heroic hero these moist Texas eyes have ever been set on."

The writer swished forward, making kissy-kissy noises with his mouth. "Hey, sailor. Want a date?"

"Bob, maybe you're right. You *are* the weirdest!" He turned his attention to the barbarian. "Sorry about my friend, Mister. I'm H.P. Lovecraft, and this is Robert E. Howard. We're ambassadors of King Henry the Eighth, going to perform our duties as diplomatic envoys to the kingdom of Prester John. How's that for some odd and exotic mishmashed historical juxtaposition. Kinda like Farmer's RIVERWORLD, only much more mythic."

"Look, buddy, knock off the old pulp crapola, you

rotten drivers are interfering with my hunting," snarled Gilganosh. "And, P.S.—could you stop this pudgy moron from humping my leg? I do an occasional sheep, but bad pulp writers just don't turn me on. Call him off, or woe unto him for the part-god Gilganosh will tear him limb from horny limb!"

"Gilganosh!" cried Robert E. Howard. "Gosh and shucks and tarnation! That's even better. Oh take me, Gilgy! Take me!"

Fortunately for the writer, Gilganosh was distracted by an attacking group of guerrillas, who tended to pop up with annoying regularity down here in Hades. Again Fortune smiled upon the writers; Howard and Lovecraft had sophisticated automatic weapons in their four by four and with the help of Gilganosh's deadly arrows, they finished the guerrillas off in no time at all.

They all went off to Prester John's, where Gilganosh and Inky-Dinky-Do beat the bejeezus out of each other and then decided to be friends once more. Lovecraft and Howard discovered publishing offices there, quit the Kingdom of Henry the Eighth and started writing sexy short stories for the Hades edition of PLAYBOY-GIRL.

In general, Bill enjoyed the stories threading through his sinuses like a bad cold, but he did wish they were longer, so he could really get more endless pleasure from the ones he liked the most, like the Goldilocks piece.

And so the days passed.

There was only one of the novels he had not read yet, and he was just starting on it, reading only the very first sentence:

ANOTHER FINE ARCHETYPICAL MYTH
by
David Pissoff

"It was a dark and stormy Nightworld"—

when suddenly the cell door banged open.

"Bang!" said the door.

"Drop your socks and grab your . . . —up and out!" shouted the commandant of the party of soldiers who stormed in the cell. "Summer camp is over and your ass is in the sling, Bill or whatever your cruddy name is," inferred the grizzled, scarred warrior, looking every inch a debilitated soldier worthy of DI-hood. "The Lord of this 'ere castle wants an audience with you and your companion! Which means like, instantly or sooner, or I stomp you to death!"

Bill smiled happily. "You think your Lord is going to let us go?"

"Let you go?" he howled in apoplectic answer. "Over my dead body—or better yours. Let you go and those two vats of boiling oil we've been stoking all day, sweating and slaving over, will go to waste!"

Bill managed to glugg down one last half-bowl of fermented swill before the soldiers dragged him out of his cell.

CHAPTER 14

THE CRIPPLED KING

"*WHAT* DID YOU SAY?"

The pitcher and goblet of wine went splashing off the table and crashing to the floor as the wild-haired Monarch of the Isthmus of Impotence dragged himself reluctantly half-way to his feet and glared down savagely with fierce blood-shot eyes at his cowering prisoners who were wrapped in heavy chains and shreds of clothing, bare blue bottoms shivering, in the midst of the audience hall. Then dropped back with a groan.

Bill licked his lips, and his heart dived with despair at the loss of all that lovely, if noticeably sour-smelling alcohol that was even now dripping onto the floor and swirling down a hair-clogged drain.

"I said, your Royal Impotence, that we are but honest

Questers after the Fountain of Hormones."

"No, no," screeched the Baron frantically, tugging at his food-spattered robes as though he was about to tear them off with excitement. "Take it back a few sentences. To the man who *sent you!*"

Bill and Rick exchanged puzzled glances. It was a fair exchange. "Well, that would be Doctor Delazny, right Bill?" said Rick, seeming noticeably paler and thinner after his forced incarceration in the dank dungeon.

"Delazny!" screeched the tall sunken eyed man as he tore out handfuls of his lank hair. "Delazny! *Him!*"

"Hey, Bill, I got the feeling, somehow, that this guy knows Delazny!"

Bill shook his head in wonderment, his chains shaking in tinkling, semi-musical accompaniment. "I got the same feeling. Only it is impossible. How could the Baron here even know about Dr. Delazny? He's a human being, sort of, and this guy some sort of archetype. Whatever that is."

Bill, in true Trooper fashion, had already forgotten most of the details of Dr. Delazny's boring lectures about archetypes. There was no room in his teeny-tiny military-shaped and alcohol-destroyed brain for the concept that the sexual dysfunction of billions of male human beings might create an archetype like this one.

The Baron moaned. A most pitiful, heart-breaking sound.

Baron Barren (for that was his name) tried to stand up from his chair but managed only a wobbling crouch. Bent and disfigured, he teetered there, growing red as a beet, tears starting from his eyes as he attempted to rise up into erect state, failing miserably.

"No, no, I am as human as you. As human as that foul beast Delazny is inhuman." Beneath swarthy, unkempt brows, glowing eyes squinted at them. He teetered there in that crouch, breathing raggedly, struggling with every ounce of his being to just stay in that one, profoundly embarrassing position. "Tell me,

Bill," Baron Barren wheezed. "Did that sodding vivi-sectionist Delazny give you that foot?"

"Not really. Actually, I got it—well—somewhere else."

Bill self-consciously tried to put the cloven hoof behind his other leg, as all the repulsive creatures in the room craned their necks and slithered closer to get a better look.

"Don't be too sure, Bill," snarled Baron Barren, pointing a ragged fingernail. "Delazny may well be at fault! The man is a pernicious fiend! Author of much, maybe all, of the wickedness in the psychosomatic research field of the Empire. They say that it was Doctor Delazny who made the Emperor's eyes strabismic during elective brain surgery to cure his ingrown toenails. If so, it is just one more mistake amidst a career of perfidy, of which we get glimmerings even here on the Isthmus, thanks to my bio-tech mechanisms!"

"How do you know Doctor Delazny?" asked Rick.

"Do you think that I have spent all my life in this contorted state? Do you think that I was *born* here in these fiendish environs? No! Can't you see . . . . Words fail me. It is so tragic! Nobody really cares. You don't care—you only asked so you can sneer at me! I was the greatest, yes I was. A respected, revered Doctor of Science of the Empire. Even you stupid creatures must have heard of me. Dr. Krankenhaus! The greatest psychosomatic surgeon in history? It was I, while performing a psycho dissection of a young male's brain, who suddenly realized the truth!"

"Truth?" Bill blinked.

"Yes!" said Baron Barren, sprays of spittle splattering from his mouth in the excitement of his oratory. "That most males think with their testicles! But no other scientist ever found the actual link! They believed that the gonads only affected the brain through the release of testosterone! But that is only partially true, and I, Dr. Krankenhaus, that fateful day at Hedshrinker U., con-

clusively proved it! It was my genius that created the
Sex-Ray—the specialized wavelength X-Ray device that
read radiation-type wave-lengths emanating from
glands. I shall never forget when I turned up the power,
and was finally able to perceive the connection that I
had only theorized before. It was a theretofore invisible
energy tube, directly connected from the nether regions
to the medulla oblongata! It was quite, quite purple in
color. And when I performed a simple bit of castration
surgery, a quick whisk of the scalpel, the tube disappeared proving that it emanated not from the brain, but
from the other end. Can't you see the importance of
that discovery gentlemen?"

"Castrated?" said Bill, his mouth dry, hands shaking,
contemplating the one true fear of the eternal macho
male.

"Oh, I sewed them back on. I was a great surgeon I
tell you! And voila! Zap! That tube reappeared again!
That tube of psychic energy! Through my further experiments I discovered that the tube also led not only
to the brain but had a branch as well through a sort of
hyper-dimensional link, a leaking psychic faucet you
might call it that dropped into a sea of human energy
that was swishing about in a different dimension! The
Over-Gland! The very land where we now stand!"

Baron Barren grew so perturbed he fell over. He did
not get up; he simply continued his lecture lying on the
floor, squirming spasmodically like a beetle on its back
when he reached the exciting bits.

"I had an assistant. Delazny! He spied on everything
I did! He soon knew everything I knew, he learned all
about the Over-Gland at almost the same instant that I
learned about it. I only wished for greater knowledge,
greater understanding of the human race, and maybe
the Galactic Nobel Prize and a nice post at Helior University. But Delazny! Little did I realize that Delazny
wanted more! Much more!"

"Yes," said Rick. "He wants to bring peace to humanity, to stop the Chinger war!"

Baron Barren snorted and writhed with disgust. "Bah! Lies! If he has joined up with the Chingers, then dollars to dung beetles he will betray them just as quickly as he betrayed the human race. For it is power that Delazny wants! Endless power! He wants to tap the cosmic energy of the Over-Gland for his own nefarious purposes! But he cannot do this until he discovers the source of that power. . . ."

"The Fountain of Hormones!" said Bill, beginning to understand the easy parts.

"Archetypically speaking, yes. The Fountain of Hormones—the nexus of this particular maelstrom. But alas, no one has ever been able to find it." He cast a wobbly gesture about him, alluding to his sorry companions. "Don't you know, if *we* could find it, we'd certainly use it. Isn't that right, you conked collection of crunched cripples?"

There was a general weak moan of agreement and a feeble thrashing amongst the assembled creatures.

"I don't understand though, Dr. Krankenhaus or Baron Barren or whatever your name is. If you are the true discoverer of the Over-Gland—then what are you doing here, and in such a sorry state!"

Dr. Krankenhaus snapped his fingers, or at least tried to snap his fingers that only slid greasily over each other, and pointed toward his captives, gurgled orders to his minions. "Let them go! And get them some trousers— I'm getting a chill just looking at their bare bums. They are as much victims as we!" As two gnomes raced forward and attended to the locks with jangling keys, Dr. Krankenhaus managed to struggle back onto his throne where he collapsed, heaving with over-exertion.

"Thanks," said Bill, pulling on the filthy fur trousers and trying to rub some circulation back onto his arms.

"You haven't answered the question," said Rick.

"No. Sorry. It hurts to even *think* about what happened." Dr. Krankenhaus's hands trembled weakly down his face as though to wash out the recollection, and yet clearly to no avail. "I am sorry to have treated you so shoddily, but it is simply the custom hereabout with potentially dangerous strangers."

"But how do you not know we aren't spies for Dr. Delazny?" asked Rick.

Krankenhaus chuckled weakly. "Spies? Hardly. You two are far too stupid for that."

"Maybe if you tell us your story, you'll feel better," prompted Bill.

"Ah yes! My story. Has ever a man endured more?"

DR. KRANKENHAUS'S STORY
Or
"Don't Crush that Pixie, Hand Me the Tweezers"

"It was late at night in the University Psych-Soma lab. I had just spent the entire evening taking readings of the Delta Smegma Hi-Fi fraternity's annual toga party, panty raid and orgy, and I was eager, as you might very well imagine, to feed the results into my computer-monitored apparatus. You see, I was in the midst of creating an energy facsimile of the 'rube tube'—that is, the psychic energy channel that conducts the energy to male brains. If this experiment worked I was certain that I could open a conduit between my machine and the Over-Gland itself. I had already created a hypothesis as to the actual energy manifestations of the Over-Gland, but I needed to actually peer inside and get a visual readout for my experiments to proceed apace.

"And what a grand experiment! What a marvelous journey it would be! To look into an as yet unfathomed X-factor in the formation of the human mind, micro to macro! I can only begin to tell you how excited I was!

"Delazny, my assistant, was supposed to have been on vacation. Little did I realize that he had manufactured a device that enabled him to tap my computer and all of my instruments in order to spy on all my activities in the lab.

"It was very late that night, and as I had not yet come home, my beautiful young daughter, Irma, brought some homebrew and porkuswine sandwiches to me. I asked her to linger for just a little while, to observe the next step in my experiments— the introduction of a small surge of energy, meant to 'prime the pump,' so to speak, to tap all of the sexual energy, which is called orgone, which I'd stored up from the toga party. I did not realize it, but Delazny's observation devices were rigged in a way to monitor these experiments as well, but Delazny, in addition to being a superhuman swine, was also a pretty rotten electrical technician. For apparently, when I pulled the lever to introduce the power surge, a goodly portion of the orgone from the toga party streamed through his wires and zapped him a half-mile away. I did not realize this—I was too absorbed in what was happening with the energy channel that had touched the Over-Gland! There was a fluctuation in the dimension planes that resulted, a warp in space! And the energies that caused it were from the other side of our dimension! What else could it be but the Over-Gland! I was on the verge of success!

"The next thing I knew, Delazny was tearing into the lab, his hair standing on end, his eyes bugging horribly, smoke streaming from his ears. 'Stand out of the way, you idiot!' he cried, making a grab for my beautiful daughter. 'I will have her! I *must* have her. Embrace! Crush! Deflower! Hot diggity-doo!'

"I must admit that I had been so involved in the course of my experiments I had not noticed the growing desire that Delazny had entertained for Irma. I became aware of it now. The charge from the Over-Gland was simply too much for him. He had to possess her there and then!

"Need I say that I fought him! We rolled around that lab while explosions banged and sparks flew. Irma tried to pull him off me, but I warned her away. Finally, we teetered at the very brink of the gateway between Here and There! I don't know where I got the strength to fight against the madman, but somehow I was able to toss him through the opening! There was a tremendous crack of energy as the hole swallowed him up. I struggled up and wrapped my arms around my precious Irma, certain that the villain was done!

"But just as I was about to turn off the energy supplying the portal, he emerged! He had clung to the sides of the portal with all the abominable strength of a madman! He climbed out from that gateway even more charged with orgone than he had been when he entered it. He roared with sexual ferocity and headed straight for Irma!

"My poor, precious daughter! Her only escape was through the portal itself and she jumped into it without a moment's hesitation rather than allow that fiend to work his evil will with her.

"And I? I was totally exhausted. I was totally enervated. Yet, somehow, with a single superhuman effort, I rallied the remaining particles of strength and seized up a chair. With it I smashed the generator and all of the most sensitive pieces of my equipment. And then, with my dear Irma's name on my lips, I fell into the doorway the very instant before it collapsed. My fall, and my total exhaustion, created the injured, useless creature that you can see before you.

"I awoke here in this Isthmus of Impotence! Ah! How fitting! The creatures in this vile place took me to be a God, and perhaps in some terrible way, I am just that! But I am a God without reason for living, for I never found my dear and precious daughter, my lovely Irma!

"And now, I am even more forlorn! For apparently

Delazny, who had no talents and was a rotten assistant besides, has apparently graduated medical school. Undoubtedly by cheating and using his charge of orgone. He is a Doctor now, and somehow—with the help of my stolen notebooks—he has recreated the Portal to the Over-Gland, sending flunkies out to search for the nexus, the very power source that will give him the wherewithal to rule the Universe! And worse, he will surely find Irma now, and have his vile way with her. Oh woe, woe, woe! Woe is me!"

Finishing his story, Baron Barren (a.k.a. Doctor Krankenhaus) dissolved into a mass of tears, blubbered sobs and quiverings.

Bill was moved. Despite years of training to avoid all forms of volunteering, while firmly believing that it was always bowb your buddy week, he stepped forward. He was touched beyond words. He stumbled up to the throne, his hand over his heart, and dropped to his knees. "Fear not, dear Dr. Krankenhaus, for I believe you with all my heart and, yea, every fiber of my being! Destiny has brought me here, has thrust us together upon this cruel shore! For I do love your daughter more than life itself! I met her, you see, when I was first tossed into the formation of the link with Over-Gland! Met her, stood aghast at her beauty, fell incontinently into the azure pools of her eyes, fell instantly, deeply, irrevocably in love with her. And truly, she loves me as, yea, I do love her!"

"Bill," said Rick bulging his eyes with horror at his suddenly possessed comrade. "Arrrr! Why the devil are you talking like that?"

Bill shook off the spell. "Sorry. The curse of the comix." He took in a deep breath. "Anyway, it's the truth, Doc. That is, if this is the same Irma." Quickly, he sketched out a description.

The effect upon the King was incredible. He had

grown paler and paler as Bill had told his tale, but now color was pumped back to his cheeks. He forced himself up into an only half-bent sitting position, his eyes glowing with some traces of renewed health and vigor. "Can it be? This is the very description of my precious, lovely Irma! You have indeed seen her."

"And it's her that I'm looking for Doc. I am, as we say in the Troopers in our own comradely way, nuts about her! I'm not really here to help Dr. Delazny, not at all! I'm here to find Irma!"

The King frowned. "I'm not really sure I want my daughter going out with a professional soldier—and one with fangs as well. No insult intended, young man. But what looks good stuck in the mush of a lion isn't exactly what I would call son-in-law material."

"Look here, Crunchy! I could get rid of the fangs you know!" snarled Bill.

"Arrrr! Bill," said Rick, agasp. "You'd give up Deathwish Drang's fangs for a woman! You really *are* in love, aren't you?"

And Bill, in a sudden excess of self-pity and indulgent lachrymose romance, found tears streaming down his cheeks. "Yes, Rick! Even I find it hard to believe that a broken down old Trooper can find love at last. But someone out there, a woman in a billion, has broken through my hard-bitten training. You know, even The Galactic Troopers of the Empire can't stop love, Rick. I will go to the farthest stars, to the very ends of the Over-Gland to find her!"

Rick shook his head. "This place has certainly had its effect on you, old friend! And not for the good, believe me. Can you *believe* that hogwash . . . ! Oh well, I'm along for the ride I guess. Love will have its way—and I have got to find that Holy Grail Ale!"

"You seek the Holy Grail Ale?" said the Baron/Doctor. "I've been looking for that myself! Great stuff, I hear. It might restore my depleted powers. You should have mentioned that before. I wouldn't have had you thrown in my dungeons."

"That's okay," said Bill. "We needed the rest anyway, didn't we, Rick?"

Rick shrugged. "I guess so." He turned to the King. "But you say that you have no idea where this Fountain of Hormones is either, Doc?"

"Alas, it is a mystery even to my instruments!"

"We met this dragon who said that it was *south*," said Bill.

"*All* roads lead south in the Over-Gland!" Baron Barren beckoned to a pair of trolls. "Lackeys! Bring my stretcher! I would show our visitors my inventions!"

Two gnarled creatures carrying a stretcher hurried up. Another helped roll the depleted Lord onto the top of it. He fell off noisily several times, making much commotion and many shrieks of rage. Babblings and scrabblings later, his constituents managed to get him balanced properly upon the stretcher, and began to haul him toward the door.

"Come along, gentlemen. Do come along. Perhaps fresh brains will help me solve this particularly twisted puzzle."

Now freed from their bonds, Bill and Rick found it quite easy to catch up with the Baron or King or Doc or whatever the hell he was, and keep pace.

"That bird around your neck, Bill," said Baron Barren. "I hesitated to mention it before. But now, since we are old buddies, you will pardon my asking. But it is almost as odd as the cleft hoof upon your leg. Am I wrong, or is that not a symbol of peace, destroyed?"

"You got it in one," Bill gloomed. "I have been stricken with the Grime of the Aging Marinator for killing the thing. I must find my true love, which is Irma, so that the spell can be lifted."

"And the foot?"

"Old war wound."

"Most interesting. But hark! We approach the chamber, a former coffee roasting room, which I have converted into my laboratory. Yes, yes, my boys. Come into my lab and see what's percolating. Har-har. Don't get much of a chance for humor around these parts."

"No," said Bill. "I guess not. Particularly if that is a sample."

"You mean you think that there might be a hope of discovering the whereabouts of the Fountain of Hormones, there in your lab?" said Rick, scratching his head doubtfully.

"Yes. In the years that I have ruled here, I have not abandoned my researches. No, only now I employ different tools. But no reason to babble on further fellows! Scritch! Pixindenda! Open those doors and take us through. Our guests are about to witness true wonder!"

Bill, who'd had more than enough of true wonder lately, would much rather have witnessed true grain alcohol; but he had to admit, this crunchy old geezer was tickling his curiosity.

Something behind that door was gurgling.

Gurgling and gulping, squirting and chugging, bellowing and hissing. It was the oddest melange of liquid sounds that Bill had heard since he had almost drowned in boot camp.

The doors to the laboratory chamber were large and solidly constructed of ironbound oak, and it was only with a great deal of grunting effort that the trolls managed to heave them open.

They then came back to pick up their master and carry him through; Bill and Rick followed, their eyes opening wider and wider as they stumbled.

"Am I seeing what I think I'm seeing?" Bill choked out.

"You're seeing it all right," Rick answered in a very hollow voice.

"What do you think?"

"I think," Rick said stepping slowly backwards, "that I am going to leave."

"Leave? You mean that *thing* bothers you?"

"Bothers me?" Rick squeaked, then swallowed heavily. "I haven't had so much fun since the pigs ate my little sister."

CHAPTER 15

THE PEPTO ABYSMAL NIGHTMARE!

"WHAT THE BOWB IS THAT?" BILL WHISpered, gulping rapidly.

Rick could only gawk and gape, his face turning a curious shade of green as though afflicted with a sudden case of gastroenteritis.

The chamber was large and high, and a full quarter of it was taken up by the Thing, not including the appendages and limbs and such that stretched down to the rudimentary control board. It was a mass of arms and ventricles and tentacles and the various organs—brains and such—that were visible through the translucent skin. As well as the usual eyes and ears popping out in unexpected places. There were also indefinable organs of various size and description, all buried in the multicolored translucent, stitched-together skin that stretched over it, or in some cases did not, exposing pulsing viscera or pumping giant hearts. In the very middle of the thing, a large eye a full yard across opened its lid and stared emotionlessly at the visitors entering its chamber.

"Behold gentlemen!" croaked Baron Barren enthusiastically. "As you have no doubt surmised by now, normal technology simply does not work here in the Over-Gland. And so I have invented bio-technology. Here before you is the first ever bio-computer. I will demonstrate."

Inspired by scientific enthusiasm, Baron Barren stumbled from his stretcher and dragged himself over to the long table, where some of the fleshy organs extended onto its surface. They were held firmly in position by levers and calipers of wood and metal. Vibrating needles showed measurements upon graphs hand drawn with neat calligraphy. Baron Barren touched a button, and at the end of a complicated organic-wood composite apparatus, ten flints struck simultaneously, lighting ten candles. By this illumination, Baron Barren assumed his Dr. Krankenhaus persona, examining the positions of the needles. "Hmmm. Things seem to be in homeostasis in the machine. I think we can call up some images now."

"Arrrr! Wait just a minute!" said Rick, finally able to speak. "Dare I presume to ask just how did you manage to create this . . . thing?"

"Foolish of me—I neglected to mention that I also hold higher degrees in advanced surgery, genetics and home TV repair. To be truthful, ho-ho, I also admit to having a bit of a reputation as an author. I supported myself through graduate school by authoring some books. I come from humble stock, my father was a Technical Fertilizer Operator—"

"My lifetime ambition!" Bill cried.

"Shut up. As I said, I have written books such as HOW TO TURN YOUR PETS INTO USEFUL

HOUSEHOLD APPLIANCES and DR. K's DO-IT-YOURSELF BRAIN TRANSPLANTS AND GASTRO-INTESTINAL SURGERY DIET. So you see I had all the necessary skills when I found myself trapped in this rotten place. I only had to round up the essential biological entities, brew up some tissue-generation vats, sharpen up some scalpels, dry out some cat-gut for stitches, then heat up some cauterizing irons. Then it was just a matter of slicing and patching together a number of creatures and rearranging an appropriate neuro-chemical system to support the bio-engineering devices necessary to my needs."

"I've never seen anything like it before!" Bill said, then pushed his popping eyes back into their sockets.

"Nor will you again," the proud inventor said. "It's a one-off. Now. Let's see what we can get on our sclera-screen." Dr. Krankenhaus pulled a lever and fumbled with a metal dial connected to a rubber band, which in turn was plugged into what appeared to be the ganglia hooked to a central nervous system.

The eye in the center of the huge patchwork beast suddenly flung its lids open. It lacked pupil and iris and instead was a uniform, grayish white right across the entire eyeball. There was a frizzle of static across the sclera, and suddenly a picture started flipping on this "eye-screen." Static-noises and garbled sound warbled from two vibrating membranes below it.

Dr. Krankenhaus did some fine-tuning, and the picture stopped rolling. An image appeared of a man standing by a table, pouring a box of something into a bowl.

"Weedies, The Breakfast of Starship Troopers," smarmed the man. "You sure as hell won't want to eat it, but it will do wonders for the hydroponics lawn in your starship's rumpus room!"

"There! You see, the Over-Gland picks up intergalactic television."

Bill's stomach flip-flopped. He remembered Weedies, all right—and so did his digestive system.

Dr. Krankenhaus turned another dial, which in turn operated a device that tweaked at a number of large teats on what appeared to be the bottom half of a black pig. The channel immediately changed. "A boob-tube!" explained the Baron happily as he noted the miffed expression on Bill and Rick's face.

There was a picture on the screen of a man holding a bottle and smiling. "Galaxative! When you really need a supernova to get that mail moving again!"

Dr. Krankenhaus spun another dial, and suddenly the picture took on a whole different character. It was much fuzzier for one thing, with only vague outlines of figures, accompanied by dim voices on the membrane speakers.

"Visual interpretation of other energy information received by the Over-Gland. And here is the area where I am presently at work, gentlemen. I believe that if I can get some better focusing on line, I can discover everything I need to find out. This is the vehicle through which I know what I know about what has happened in the Empire since I was exiled by Delazny."

"And what about this puzzle you mentioned," said Rick. "Exactly what is it?"

"Why, the exact location of the Fountain of Hormones, of course! The exact place which is the source of power here! If it was *easy* to find, do you not think that I would be utilizing it already? If it was easy to locate, do you not think that Dr. Delazny would already be tapping it to obtain the power he needs to rule the universe?"

"But why is it a puzzle?" asked Bill.

"Ah! Because the nature of the very laws of physics and mathematics are twisted here in the Over-Gland. Allow me to show you! Trolls! Brings me out my chalkboard and my mathematical charts!" Quickly, the trolls hopped to it, rolling out the desired boards on squeaky wheels until they were within reach of the bent Dr. Krankenhaus. The Baron-Doctor picked up a pointer and a piece of chalk.

"Now, gentlemen, the thing is that the mathematics looks much the same as it does in normal reality, but it functions under more bio-chemical principles . . . since this is, after all, just one great big psycho-gland we're in. Now, I've explored this, and I've renamed the tools appropriately."

His pointer tapped a large zero on the chart.

"Now this in our understanding is called a 'Zero,' correct? Well, here, in Over-Gland Mathematics, we call it 'Zero' as well, but we mean 'Z.E.R.O.,' standing for 'Zenithial Entry Retro Orifice.' Naturally, the female principle of glandular mathematics! And numbers—1, 2, 3, 4, 5, and so on are called 'members'—or rather, I should say 'integers' are called 'intercourses' or, well, something like that. Anyway, when you put these 'intercourses' in any parenthetical group containing one or more 'Z.E.R.O.' there is automatic 'multiplication' or 'spawning.' This glandular variation on the 'set theory' is naturally called the 'sex theory.'"

Dr. Krankenhaus began to chalk up numbers on the board.

"God, I'd hate to find out what 'division' is, Bill," said Rick.

"Now the result of this spawning," said Dr. Krankenhaus, chalking up an equals sign, "is 'fractions' of course, and here is where we enter the nether world or 'quantum mechanics,' which I call 'scrotum mechanics' here in the Over-Gland.

"Now, if you have followed my arguments closely one thing should be perfectly clear by now. The essence of glandular physics! In the end, it just doesn't make any sense!" He pulled down a chart upon which were an innumerable quantity of strange mathematical chicken-scratchings.

"Here, gentlemen are my equations on the subject! Supposedly, the end result should be the exact coordinates of the nexus point, the nucleus of the Over-Gland! The so-called Fountain of Hormones which we all seek! The trouble is that each time I run this through my bio-computer here, I get a different set of co-ordinates here, because the goddamn 'members' always get together with the 'Z.E.R.O.s' and throw some new fractions into the soup!" He shook his head wearily. "Well, now that I've explained all this to you, Bill and Rick. . . . Any idea about what the solution to the puzzle might be? Think of what success will mean! It will heal me and restore vitality to the Isthmus of Impotence. We'll both see Irma again, Bill, and Rick—well, I'm sure somewhere in the Fountain you'll find your Holy Grail Ale!"

Bill stared blankly at the equations, scratching his head. Then he looked over at the bio-computer, which was cranking and chunking away, making all sorts of rude biological noises in the process. "I can add and subtract, and maybe multiply and divide a little if I'm not too tired. Sorry, Doc. Or Baron. Or whatever. It's got me stumped. I guess Rick and I are just going to have to hit the trail again and start looking."

"Not necessarily!" said Rick.

Both Bill and Dr. Krankenhaus swung their heads his way. Even the bio-computer made a squelching kind of "Hunh?" and blinked its eye.

"You have an idea?" whispered Krankenhaus, voice filled with desperate hope.

Rick had a strange, silly grin on his face. His eyes sparkled unnaturally. His teeth seemed to glint. With heroism? Or with something else—

"These equations, Doctor," said Rick, stepping forward and tapping the charts. "They're quite fascinating. A breakthrough, in fact, in non-linear mathematics, to say nothing of non-Euclidian geometry."

"You understand higher math?" asked Dr. Krankenhaus eagerly.

"Arrrr! This and that," said Rick obtusely. "But more importantly, I learned math, Doctor, from a beautiful gymnast/mathematics tutor at Organism University. And Doctor, I was tutored in action!" He pointed out one equation in particular. "Positions, Doctor! You have entirely neglected to *factor* in the importance of positions to this glandular mathematics. It's all too easy to slip into pure theory. But in glandular mathematics, there's nothing like *experience*."

"I don't understand."

"It's very simple. Just add one number to all these equations, and you'll get the correct coordinates every time."

"And what number, pray tell, is that?"

Rick cleared his throat and nodded grimly. "Why, '69', of course."

The dilapidated Doctor's mouth dropped onto his chest.

His assistants rushed forward and pushed and pulled and helped him get his mouth back into place. "This happens from time to time," he apologized to his guests. "An excellent idea, Rick. Let's feed it into the computer!"

With wild enthusiasm Bill and Rick hurled the chalkboard and charts aside, then kicked them into one of the several large mouths of the organic computer. The mouth closed and started to chew on the information with the oversized molars that Bill had only glimpsed.

"Arrr!" said Rick. "Talk about 'number-crunching.'"

"We're getting an answer!" said Dr. Krankenhaus, looking up from his mechanical read-outs. "I don't believe it, gentlemen, but it's actually working! It's coming up with coordinates that are not variables.... Trolls! Quickly! The maps!"

More charts were wheeled into the room. These looked like maps made by a maniac bombed out on dope, but Dr. Krankenhaus seemed to know his way around them. He riffled through a pile, tore off some, and finally emitted a shriek of triumph! "I found it! I found the location of the Fountain of Hormones!"

"Arrrr! So give! Where is it?"

The Doctor-Baron fumbled his way out of the layers of maps, clutching one sheet in his contorted hand. A gnarled fingernail was pointed at a spot on the map, and his eyes popped out with surprise.

This time the trolls stuck a handle into the side of his head and wound his eyeballs back into place. As soon as he could see again the good doctor pulled the map to him more, then held it out, tremblingly, to Bill and Rick.

It looked like no other map they had ever seen before. In fact, it looked more like a fine collection of pornographic woodcuts. "There it is!" cried Dr. Krankenhaus, pointing to a dark, smeary part of the map.

"Okay, Doc," said Bill. "I give up. Just where is that?"

Dr. Krankenhaus shook his head, his face still filled with surprise. "It's here, don't you understand? Right *here* where we are standing!"

CHAPTER 16

INTO THE
MALE-FEMALE-STROM

"HERE?" GASPED BILL.

"Here!" gurgled Rick, his eyes fairly glowing with excitement.

"Yes indeed. According the figures that the bio-computer has given us, the Fountain of Hormones, the very nexus of the Over-Gland, is right here in this castle!"

"That doesn't make any sense," said Bill. "This is the Isthmus of Impotence. What would it be doing here?"

"It must be latent . . . potential energy on the outskirts of nascent being . . ." mumbled Baron-Krankenhaus uncertainly.

"No, nothing latent about glandular energy, people!" cried Rick with great enthusiasm. "We're talking biology here, Doc. We're talking *chemistry*. If we can imagine the Over-Gland to be rather like a supra-dimensional amoeba, then its nexus would be like an amoeba's nucleus, floating within its mass. Clearly, the Fountain of Hormones has chosen this spot for a very specific reason."

"But where is it?" said Bill. "I don't see any Fountain."

"Then that may only be a metaphorical term, Bill," said Rick. "But I submit, Doctor, that at this very instant there are biological devices manufacturing hormones at an incredible rate, even as we speak."

"Exhaustion grips me," the drooping doctor droned, staggering and almost falling. "My brain cells don't seem to connect very well. Could you—would you—explain?!"

Rick pointed at the bio-computer. "Delighted to, Doctor. When you sewed all those bodies together, you must have included all their glands, including of course those involved with the sexual process. It is my theory, hopefully soon to be proved, that they have all moved, all melded together into one super-sex organ that is now attached to the sophisticated nervous system of the computer. The energies they've given off must have attracted every other energy source." Rick was dancing with excitement. "This is it! This computer is the tap for all the sexual energy of the known universe! And maybe some parts still unknown!"

"Young man," said Baron Krankenhaus. "I must say you seem to know a *great* deal about not only glandular mathematics and sexual mechanics—indeed, you seem to comprehend whole areas beyond even *me!*"

Rick ignored the comment as he rushed to the controls. "Mere theorizing, Doc. What we have to do is to test it out! If we have the correct idea, then possibly we'll be able to use these instruments here to tap the Fountain—which in turn controls the Over-Gland. And what is the one thing you both desire for different reasons?"

"A drink?" asked Bill, licking his lips.

"No, bowbhead—forgotten already? Your heart's desire, Bill. Irma, of course."

"Irma!" the doctor cried aloud, a heartfelt wail of woe. "Yes, of course! My dear, lovely daughter. Yes, she floats in the Over-Gland, and it was there that Bill met her. Yes! If we can program her vital statistics in, we might well be able to pull her out!"

"38–22–34!" said Bill.

"How could you possibly know my daughter's measurements, Bill?" asked the Doctor-Baron, astounded.

"I just happened to hear, somewheres," Bill muttered—then quickly changed the subject. "So what are you waiting for, Rick? Program the vital statistics!"

"With your permission, Doctor."

"Of course! Oh, could my seemingly endless quest for my daughter be at an end at last? How long have I been searching? Centuries, it seems. Go Rick, go! But, by the way, just in passing, your speech patterns seem somehow very familiar to me. Haven't I met you somewhere before?"

"Here we go, Doc!" Rick exulted, ignoring the question and getting to work with the controls.

"Wait a minute! How do you know how to do that?"

"I'm a fast study," said Rick, pushing levers and buttons. Tendons twitched, nerves and ganglia sparkled and snapped with electrochemical energy.

"Zoroaster!" said Bill, alarmed. "What's happening to the bio-computer?"

A shimmer of light rippled across the mottled, translucent, stitched together skin of the gargantuan thing. It shook and it spasmed, as though undergoing the most profound and uncomfortable internal rearrangement.

"Yes!" cried Rick. "And now here we go—38–22–34! Come on, baby. We want Irma Krankenhaus!"

The eye of the bio-computer was fluttering open and

closed as though in the midst of a complex drug trip. Tongues fluttered out from the multitude of mouths like New Year's Eve joymakers. Bulges began to grow along the massive skin, like inflating balloons.

Then, with an internal groan, a body could be seen appearing inside one of these elongated swellings, a face and body stretching the membrane.

"Anybody got a pin?" said Rick.

However, a pin proved unnecessary. This new stretched membrane popped of its own accord, sending out a splatter of fluid onto the floor, the drenched woman slipping and sliding along with it.

Bill could not believe his eyes. "Irma!" he cried joyously. "Irma!"

"Yuck!" cried the woman, floundering on the floor. "Don't just stand there, you idiot! Help me get out of this mess—I'm dripping wet!"

Gingerly, Bill stepped forward, and pulled Irma up into his embrace. He didn't mind the water at all—in fact he enjoyed the way it rendered Irma's previously translucent gown almost invisible. "Irma! Do you recognize me?"

"Of course I recognize you, lamebrain. You're Bill, and I'm the love of your life. Now would someone kindly tell me just where the hell am I? All I know is I'm *not* in a very good mood."

She looked around at Rick, and registered nothing. But then she turned and saw Baron Barren, head bobbling with anticipation, looking hopefully and happily at her.

"Daddy!" she cried, pulling herself away from Bill. "Daddy!" She went over to the man and hugged him. "Daddy," she said, pulling away and examining him appraisingly. "Has your arthritis been acting up again?"

"It's a long story, honeybun. It's just good to see you again, that's all."

"And look!" cried Bill, staring down at his chest. The dead dove and leather thong were disappearing! "I've found you, and the Grime of the Aging Marinator is going away! I'm freed of the curse! Can life actually be a story that has a happy ending?" Bill ran to his beloved and swept her up in his arms, planting a kiss on her lips.

"Happy ending?" said Rick. "Why yes, I think so, Bill. But probably not for you, or the Doctor, or Irma— or for that matter, the universe!"

Bill, Irma still locked in his embrace, turned and looked at his erstwhile companion. Rick had a strange look of satisfaction on his face—and his color had changed again. Now it looked rather gray. Almost a *metallic* gray.

"Oh, no! How could I have been such a fool!" said Baron Krankenhaus. "I should have seen what was coming! Trolls, stop him! Kill him!"

The trolls stumbled and hurtled forward to the attack. But not quickly enough, no indeed. The Supernal Hero's hands flew across the controls of the computer. Microseconds later, two of the bio-computer's mouths opened. Long tongues flickered out, wrapped themselves around the trolls and pulled them into the fiercely gnashing mouths.

Rick laughed maniacally. "I've found it! The Fountain of Hormones! The nexus! The center to the power that I have always craved!"

"Rick?" said Bill. "Rick, old buddy. Are you maybe going slightly nuts? I know that every week is Bowb-Your-Buddy Week but this is ridiculous!"

"Oh no!" rasped Dr. Krankenhaus. "Oh God, no! It *can't* be! Guards! Fiends! Creatures! *Help!*"

"Save your breath, Doc," exulted Rick, his voice noticeably different now. "I took the precaution of bolting, locking and then *supergluing* —" He held up a container with a dripping nozzle, "—the doors here! And since I've already mastered the controls on this corpuscular computer, a little nudge. . . ." Rick flicked a toggle. Immediately, a chorus of muffled screams filtered through the thick doors. ". . . will take care of any battering ram attempts. That was the psychic equivalent of a quick knee in the groin, my friends. So stay where you are or be prepared for a good swift one as well!"

"Rick! What's wrong with you!" said Bill, baffled.

"That's the voice of Latex Delazny," said Irma. "I recognize it."

"Irma, I meant to ask you," said Bill. "How come you told me your name was Irma Feritele?"

"I don't know, Bill. I guess I lost my memory. I got confused." She jabbed a finger at Rick. "But I can't forget that voice. Delazny! This is all *your* fault!"

"I've come to your succor, haven't I, sweet Irma? And I still mean to have you, my love . . ." A leer crept over Rick's contorted features, ". . . and every other beautiful woman in the Galaxy to boot. I'll show those fools—how they sneered at me—what macho really means!"

"But Rick . . . Buddy! What happened? Have you been on dirty Delazny's side all along?" said Bill, feeling betrayed.

"Can't you see, Bill?" gasped Dr. Krankenhaus. "That's not Rick the Supernal Hero! That's an android model. Controlled, no doubt, by sophisticated radio signals by Dr. Delazny himself, safely hiding away somewhere *outside* the Over-Gland!"

"That's right, Bill! I built this model special myself!" came Delazny's voice through Rick's mouth. "And it all worked out very well! I knew you were my man, Bill! I just knew your homing instincts would take us right to where the hormones hang out! And now, thanks to this wonderfully bizarre contraption that the good Doctor has built—with a few special settings that I will set into it right now—I will be able to control the bio-computer from my base beneath the sea at Colostomy!"

"I don't understand, Delazny!" said Bill. "Just what the bowb are you trying to do? I thought you were seeking the secrets of peace! I thought you were trying to stop the Chinger War!"

"Oh, the War will stop soon enough! With this new power I will be able to crush anyone or anything that gets in my way! And naturally, I shall control every single human being in the Universe! I shall have power that no other tyrant has ever dreamed of! Every man my slave—and much more important, every woman as well. All of them mine! Mine! They all laughed and said I was mad!" The Rick android cackled wildly. "Now we'll see who is mad! Do excuse me for a moment. I have some rather important adjustments to make!" The android turned back to diddle with the knobs and switches on the board.

"No!" cried Dr. Krankenhaus. "No, I won't allow it!" Somehow, the man untwisted himself and commenced staggering toward the Dr. Delazny creature, his hands out and curled into claws. "I'll kill you, Delazny! Kill you!"

The Rick android grinned, and pulled a switch. With a horrendous scream, Dr. Krankenhaus vibrated for a moment, and then crashed to the floor, twitching and spasming until he passed out.

"Daddy!" cried Irma.

"Stay back," said Bill, grabbing ahold of her and keeping her from running to her wounded father.

A pseudopod from the bio-computer flowed out and enveloped the fallen doctor. It pulled him through an opening in the thing's side.

"Ha ha ha! Now stay back, you two," warned Rick/Delazny. "I have a vile purpose in mind for you both, for which I will need you alive. . . . But if you try anything, I'll be just as happy to feed you to the Bio-Comp here!" He turned back to the controls, playing them with manic skill, laughing all the while.

Irma fell into Bill's arms, sobbing and moaning. "Daddy!" she cried. "Oh, dear Daddy! I've lost you forever."

Bill enjoyed holding onto her—but realized as well that this was the time for cool thought, not warm embrace. What could he do? Trying to stop the android at the controls would clearly deliver him into a fate as unsavory as that of the late Dr. Krankenhaus. Irma's warm, soft body against his was most distracting. But— was this the end?

"Psst!" said a tiny little whisper. "Bill!"

Bill blinked. "Wussha?"

What was that? Surely not Irma down there, snuffling and sobbing into his manly chest. No, it didn't sound like her at all! Maybe it was his imagination.

"Psst!" That voice again. "Bill! Bill, down here!" It was from the floor! "Your foot, Trooper. Lift up your foot?"

"Which one?" said Bill.

"The cloven one, you idiot! I've got to talk to you!"

Bill shrugged. It was something to do. "Excuse me, Irma," he said, gently pushing her away. "My foot wants to talk to me. Could you keep me standing while I lift it up."

"The strain," Irma sobbed. "I can understand, it was too much for you. Something snapped. But, dearest Bill, you're all I've got now."

"Look, can we talk about this later. Just let me lean on your shoulder."

She nodded moistly through her tears, holding him so he wouldn't fall while he lifted his bare foot up. His joints crackled and he could barely lift it high enough to reach his chest, but he bent his head down to meet it halfway.

"What do you want?" he whispered to his foot.

"Gee—don't you recognize my voice, Bill?" said the foot.

"Bgr the Chinger!" Bill cried out.

"Not so loud! Delazny will notice!"

"What are you doing in my *foot*?" Bill visualized the interior of his foot with a set of controls, screens, a water-cooler—just like back on board the CHRISTINE KEELER.

"Gee, I'm not in your foot, dummy. I planted a two-way TV-radio transmitter in the crack in your cloven hoof, just in case. Good thing, too. Delazny's got me and all the other Chingers imprisoned back here at the base. Mission: Peace through the Over-Gland is, I must admit it, a total bust, Bill. We've got to stop this maniac, or both Chingers and human beings will be kaput!"

"Tell me about it! But what am I supposed to do? One wrong move and I'm zapped. Or eaten for breakfast by the computer."

A loud voice interrupted Bill's intimate tête-à-tête with his foot. "What's up, Bill? What kind of hanky-panky you up to over there standing on one leg! Is the strain telling?"

"Yes, well— ahh, indeed," said Bill, completely at a loss for words.

"Not good enough, Bill," the Chinger hissed. "Gee, but you are dumb. Give him an excuse. Tell him you're *praying!*"

"Praying!" said Bill, shouted. "It's a kind of real old form of Zoroastrian prayer, Doctor. I'm making my peace with my God. That okay with you?"

"Oh! Sure. Sorry. Never want to come between a man and his stupid superstitions. Seen one god, you've seen them all," Rick/Delazny muttered as he went back to work on the controls.

Irma was watching all this with a clamped-shut mouth and wide eyes, straining with every erg of energy she was capable of erging to keep Bill from falling on his face.

"Now what?" asked Bill. "Tell me what to do!"

"I never thought you would ask! Fortunately, my mentally debilitated friend, I have also planted a micro-grenade right by the radio. You got that?"

"To blow me up or what!" Bill asked, instantly filled with suspicion.

"Gee—Bill, what kind of an old buddy do you think I am? We go back a long ways! I would be hurt, Bill,

by that accusation. If I had human emotions. Which I
don't. So let's get on with. No, it's not to nuke you,
of course not. It's for you to use, in a jam like this!
Foresight I believe it is called."

"Things are bad, but not bad enough to commit su-
icide. You can't ask me to do it!"

"No, no, bowb-for-brains! I don't want you to kill
yourself. Just dig the thing out first, huh? Slide the right
half of the hoof off . . . I made it like a false heel."

"Okay. Right," said Bill, obeying the instructions.
Hopping about and crunching Irma at the same time,
he grabbed the hoof and pulled hard. Half of the bottom
slid off, easy as you please. A little round ball, with a
button sticking out fell out into Bill's palm.

"Now what?" said Bill.

"First you press the Button. Then—"

Bill pressed the button.

"No! Not *now* you idiot!" screeched the voice.
"You've only got eight seconds before it blows!"

"What'll I do?" Bill said, frantically. The little black
ball was *sizzling*! It didn't sound promising, not at all.

Rick/Delazny wheeled around. "What's going on
over there?" He demanded. "Am I hearing things—or
do I recognize that voice! A Chinger voice. Bgr! What
are you doing here?"

"Hurry up, Bill! We've got to destroy the bio-
computer. Lob the micro-grenade."

But Bill's attention was on the android's hand, reaching down to the destruct switch that would sizzle him.
He groaned in fretful, anticipation. This was the end.

"Never! No!" Bill cried aloud, and hurled the mini-
grenade directly at Rick/Delazny.

"Fool!" cried Doctor Delazny. "You can't stop me
now. You can't—"

The mini-grenade landed directly in Rick/Delanzy's
wide-open mouth, rattled down its throat and landed
with a clang in its metallic stomach.

"Oh no!" he sighed. "Stop me if I am wrong. But,

is it possible, that I just swallowed a mini-grenade?"

"No," said Bill. "Actually it was a *micro*-grenade!"

"Four seconds, Bill!" warned Eager Beager. "You had better do something, or you'll all be blown into a cloud of glowing atoms. That's a wicked mother of a grenade!"

The android was already groping at the control board when Bill hurled himself across the room. He caught the arm just as the fingers were about to pound upon the relevant switch. His mighty farmboy thews, Trooper training improved, strained against his enemy's weight. Bill's shirt burst open as his mighty muscles tensed—and it was working! Not only was the android Rick stopped from touching the controls, he was lifted inches off the ground.

"Two seconds, Bill!" cried his foot.

Panicked, Bill looked wildly about for a way out.

Only one existed.

"Open wide, bio-comp!" he said, picking up the squirming android with his two right arms, and sighting along his body. Gasping with the effort he ran forward and chucked Rick and the embedded micro-computer directly into the thing's mouth.

"Now run, Bill!" cried the radio-voice of Eager Beager.

"But there's no place to run *to*!" said Irma.

"One second!"

Bill grabbed Irma and headed for the furthest corner. They almost reached it.

Imagine the sound that a star might make if it were made of cream cheese and bologna when it novaed. This was somewhat the sound that the exploding bio-computer made.

The air filled with flying strips of flesh, gallons of splattering gore. A fine red mist hung in the air, like a ground cloud of beet juice, when Bill managed to struggle to his feet and looked around at the carnage.

"Not nice," said Bgr.

"Yuck!" said Irma.

"That wasn't at all friendly, Bill!" said the head of Rick, rolling about on the floor.

Before Bill could respond a strong current of some implacable ethereal force seized him, pulling him and Irma from the corner of the chamber.

"Bill, what's happening?" Irma screamed questioningly.

Bill thrashed up and turned toward the center of the room, getting exactly one second's worth of a glimpse of their unfortunate destiny.

Like a swirling spiral galaxy, sparklers of thrashing energy had popped into being where the bio-computer had once been. These were spinning like a pinwheel, causing a malevolent maelstrom in the air.

Then Bill was pulled down again, and his consciousness got mixed up with the sparklers and blackness below.

CHAPTER 17

OLD TROOPERS NEVER DIE;
THEY JUST SMELL
THAT WAY

DOWN THROUGH THE YEARS, IN WHAT some might call a checkered career, though he rarely played checkers, since being forcefully inducted into the Imperial Troopers, Bill had had many near-death experiences.

In any case, in all of the close calls, close encounters of the repulsive kind, in all the near-death experiences he'd ever had, this was definitely the most unedifying.

Bill dreamed, oh how he dreamed!, that he was frolicking frenetically in a gigantic beer mug with a dozen nubile women. One of the voluptuous women was Irma, who was sitting on top of a soggy potato chip, beckoning to him like a siren. Bill admired all the other gorgeous creatures who were frolicking about him, but rejected their sultry advances and breast-stroked instead toward Irma.

It was difficult indeed to ignore the others, but in his heart-of-hearts he knew that he was now a one-woman-Trooper, and so he swam the rest of the way, ignoring temptation. He clambered up the potato chip, which soggily bent and crumbled under his weight, closer ever closer to the smiling, beckoning Irma.

"Here, Bill," she said in a sweet, huskily sensuous voice. "Come here and kiss me, lover!"

In his death-dream, Bill knew that this contained all that was beautiful and mysterious in Love. All that he'd yearned for all this time was in this proffered smooch; life and death, fire and ice, yin and yang; even the code for his Captain Cosmos Secret Decoder Ring. Here was life's Promise; here was Destiny's Call; here was what all these frustrated pent-up feelings gnawing at his innards were for!

"Oh, Irma!" he said passionately, reaching for her.

Her lips blossomed into a pink blossom of ecstasy.

Closing his eyes, he puckered up and fell toward her, surrendering his heart, his body, his soul, his hopes for Heaven and his Phigerinadon salamander-tail collection.

But instead of moist, delicious, tender lips—

Reality did a belly-flop, death retreated, and Bill landed hard and headfirst on his mush on the ground, getting a mouthful of grit and sand for his trouble.

"Pfuiii!" he said, opening his eyes. They were gummed with grit. He wiped them and spat out a gobful of sand. Coughing, he managed to pull himself up into a half-crouch, peering uncertainly about him, trying to get a finer focus on this particular glandscape tune-in.

Bill sat plumb in the middle of a large stretch of desert. It looked a lot like the stuff that Great-Great-Grandfather Bill had bought on Phigerinadon last century, when he took his family to that colony planet: valuable beach-front property, without the beach. (Fortunately, they relocated to more fertile territory, but at a cost of what little money they had, resulting in generation after generation of the same penury that Bill had inherited.) As far as Bill could see (which wasn't too far—there was still a lot of grit in his eyes) cactus and sagebrush stretched out to the distant horizon. Occasionally, a tumbleweed rolled along, pushed by a melancholy, sighing desert wind. Up ahead were jagged, majestic mountains, capped by snow. In the near distance, a sign by a snaking road tilted precariously.

Bill groaned and rubbed his head. Then he got up and did a quick inventory of all the important body parts. The presence of his head and legs was already established; a quick examination proved that his hands were still intact, and that, yes, he still had a cloven hoof for a foot. However, instead of the rags he had worn before, he was now dressed in denim jeans, chaps and a red checked flannel shirt, loosely surrounded by a leather vest. Around his waist was a belt, leather as well, and upon this belt was a holster, containing an antique firearm which, possibly, might be a six-shooter revolver.

Upon his head was a ten-gallon, Texas Ranger hat.

Bill recognized all his gear from the days of his first stumbling literacy. While his speaking vocabulary had been severely limited, his reading skills then, like most of his peer group, and possibly now, were next to zilch. Which is why all comic books had verbal outputs that talked to the reader when he turned the page. Which meant that the idiot reader didn't have to read CRUNCH, CRASH or BANG since they sounded out tinnily from the page. In those days TALES FROM THE OLD GALACTIC WEST had been one of his favorite three-dee eye-screamers.

Which was fine for the past—but what the bowb was

he doing now, in this strange yet familiar place? He took off his hat and examined it.

And what was a six-limbed, seven-inch tall lizard doing inside his new ten-gallon hat?

"Hi there, Bill! Gee, it's sure good to see you're still alive, old hoss." The Chinger waved his tiny hands in greeting, and then hopped down to the ground, where he made a pot-hole in the sand. (Bill wondered why he'd not been crushed to the ground with the incredibly dense animal on his head; then put the thought aside for the moment since there were a few more pertinent things to wonder about now than that.)

"Bgr the Chinger! What are you doing here? And by the way, just *where* is *here*, anyway?"

"Can't you tell, Bill! It's the Mythical Great American West of Old Earth! The stuff that dreams are made of."

Bill shook his head. "Old Earth is just a legend . . . er . . . oh!" He snapped his fingers. "I get it! This is like, a part of the Over-gland!"

"Not only a *part*, it would seem Bill," said Eager Beager, hopping around excitedly. "It would seem to be the actual *base*! The *phor* below the *meta*—or should it be the opposite way around? No matter . . . I'll ask Delazny before I blow him all the way to the unhappy hunting grounds."

Bill could see that Bgr was dressed in miniature Western garb as well, down to tiny spurs and two tiny Colt .45s, which he was spinning fancily with two hands, the thumbs of his other two hands hooked into his cartridge belt. "Hey, watch it with those guns, guy!" said Bill. "What happened, anyway? Last I remember, we were getting sucked into the hole that was left after the Fountain of Hormones blew!"

"Gee—you got a great memory, pardner. That explosion—well done, by the way, Bill—reached out and clobbered Delazny's machines on Colostomy IV—and sucked him and me and the whole crew of the complex into the Male-Female-Strom in the bargain! Apparently, once more our destinies are interwoven, Bill! I ended up here, with you!"

Bill blinked rapidly as his groggy brain cells labored for comprehension. Thinking can be a painful process. "Right," he finally said smiling with understanding. Then frowning with unhappiness, "But I've lost Irma again!"

"Oh no, you haven't, podner! Look over there!"

Bill looked in the direction that the Chinger was pointing. Behind a particularly large cactus, he noticed the flutter of cloth, a protruding shoe.

"Well I'll be hornswaggled!" Bill shouted, whooping and yipping and tossing his hat into the air. "It's Irma." A befuddled expression crept onto his features. "Now, why'd I say that? What's a hornswaggle?"

"Best not to ask, friend Bill. It's undoubtedly a bit of the Wild West idiom. The argot! The overlay of trans-positional quasi-reality in the Gland-core affects us all that way. Hence the duds, you see!" He preened in his own outfit, which sparkled with spangles.

"Irma!" Bill hurried over past sagebrush and cacti, to retrieve his fallen paramour. Unconscious, she was lying demurely on a large rock. And surprise of surprises, for the first time since Bill had met her, she was modestly dressed! She wore a long, gaily colored frock, and a hat heavily plumed with feathers. On her feet were tasteful cowgirl boots.

Coiled comfortably on her always impressive bosom was a rattlesnake.

"Tarnation!" said Bill. "Bgr . . . It's some kind of a serpent. What kind?"

Eager Beager whipped out a little book labeled LOST CHINGER'S GUIDE TO THE OLD WEST.

"Gee—Bill. There are a lot of them. Kingsnake. Hoopsnake. Snake-in-the-Grass. Reckon that might be a rattlesnake. Does it have any rattles?"

The snake lifted its head somnolently, slipped its tongue in and out—and rattled its rattles nastily.

"A rattlesnake indeed! Just like it says in the book. And, PS, it also says that it is extremely dangerous and poisonous."

"Do something!"

"Gee, Bill. Ever since that traumatic experience back on Veneria when I got swallowed by one, well, you see, I kind of shy away from snakes. I think I'll go over and rustle up some chow. You've got a gun. Tarnation, son. Just blast and shoot the gol' blasted thing!" The Chinger seemed pleased as punch with his new Wild Western persona. He waddled bowleggedly back to the campsite, leaving Bill alone with Irma and the sinister rattlesnake.

The snake wiggled its tail again. Bill had no doubt at all that it really was a rattlesnake. The noise woke Irma. She fluttered her pretty eyelashes. "Gosh alive!" she said, breathlessly. "Where am I?"

"Just set tight there, Irma. Don't move a muscle! I'll save you." Bill drew his gun and examined it. The thing wasn't at all like a blaster, where you just pointed it in a general direction and pressed a stud. No, it looked like you had to aim it. And the projectiles—Bill supposed that they emerged from the metal nozzle here.

Irma took one look at the snake and fainted dead away.

And this long curved thing, Bill supposed, was the trigger. Yes, his comic book reading was coming back to him. He pointed the gun and pulled the trigger. There was a tremendous explosion, expectoration of smoke and Bill was knocked flat on his back by the recoil.

When he struggled up, there was the plume of purplish smoke dissipating in the air, and bits of flesh and snake-hide splattered over sagebrush and sand.

"Hey!" said Bill. "I guess I'm a pretty good shot with this thing." He spun the gun expertly by the trigger guard as he slipped it back into its holster.

The explosion had woken Irma up. Shock slowly dissolved from her features. "Bill. You saved me! Again!"

Bill grinned. "A man's gotta do what a man's gotta do!"

"Bill, where are we? Why am I dressed this way?"

Bill was unbuckling his belt.

"Bill, why are you undressing that way?"

"A man's gotta do what a man's gotta do!"

"Oh Bill! My hero! Do it, man!"

Finally! thought Bill. Finally his heart's desire . . . to say nothing of the desire of other portions of his anatomy.

"Gee, Bill. Sorry to disturb what appears to be an imminent and highly interesting human fertility ritual!" squeaked the too-familiar voice of Bgr. "But there's a stagecoach a-coming this way. Maybe we can hitch a ride! So could we have a rain check on the ritual? But do let me know when you plan to indulge in it again. I want to take notes."

"Eeeek!" squeaked Irma, springing gracefully up off the ground and hiding behind her hero. "Bill! It's another reptile! Shoot it, Bill. Shoot it!"

Bill scowled at Bgr the Chinger. "Sure would like to oblige, ma'am. But that there's Bgr! He might just be able to help get us out of this here fix." Bill spat on the ground. "He sure as hell got me into it! And, no, you can't watch next time."

"C'mon, people. Hurry! We gotta catch that coach!" Bgr scampered off, and they followed.

"Gee—isn't this just great, Bill?" said the Chinger, hanging onto the bouncing seat so hard that his fingers dug deep into the wood.

The stagecoach rocked and swayed as its four-strong team of horses pulled it along the rutted desert trail. He and Bill rode shotgun on top of the coach, seated beside the grizzled, sunburnt old coot named Alf Bob Barker, who smelled like a wet goat. Irma was in the passenger section of the coach below, along with the other passengers. The sun was creeping downwards through the azure sunset toward the horizon—like a brass coin falling towards a dusty desert destiny.

No, thought Bill. It wasn't great, not at all. His innards felt like they were being stirred by an ax handle, then wrapped around a spiny cactus. Or something like that.

"The fresh desert air! The smell of the wilderness! The scent of leather! The feel of honest clothes on one's hide!" enthused the Chinger.

"Shut up, Chinger, or I *will* shoot you!" said Bill.

The coach that had picked them up was headed for Mulch Gulch Falls, or that was what the driver claimed anyway. Bill had absolutely no idea what the significance of that town might be in terms of any cosmic happenings that might be controlling their destiny. All he wanted to do was get off this primitive travel apparatus which was just a new kind of torture machine. And get a cold and hopefully alcoholic drink down his dust-filled throat. And after that—Irma!

Ah, yes! Finally, he had found her. His heart fluttered dyspeptically even as his stomach churned.

The old codger to his side chomped messily on his wad of tobacco, and then shot a squirt of brown saliva from the side of his mouth. "Yep!" he said. "Sure a good thing I ran across you people out there in the desert! Mulch Gulch Falls is a fur piece from there, and that's a mighty thirsty trek, yes sirree, bob!"

"We certainly appreciate the ride, Mister. Being as we don't have any money and all."

"You got a gun, that's ticket enough." Another tobacco splat, this jet blinding a gopher peering out of its hole. "Lost my shotgun man, Jeb Hawkins, just last week to Injuns. Apaches. Done filled him so full of arrows, coulda doubled for a porcupine! Yep, and I need a gun by my side, being as Ah'm headed for the roughest town in the territory."

"Mulch Gulch? A tough town?" Bill parroted nervously.

"You betcha! That's where the baddest bunch of out-laws west of the Messasucki hang out."

"Gee—and who would that be, Mister?" asked Bgr.

"Cute little toy ya got there, partner. Like your vent-tree-lo-quism act, too." Alf Bob scratched his buttocks and then tossed out a whip tip at the back of a lagging horse, neatly picking off a large horsefly at the same time. "Anyway, that would be Frank and Jesse Jism, folks. None other than the notorious Jism Gang. They just keep on riding into town, shooting up the town—and then forcibly dee-posit their ill-gotten gains into the First Fiduciary Fertility and Ovum Bank of the Wyoming territory. They just get the biggest kick out of injecting their loot into that bank, rather than robbing it! It's all for fun, anyway—'cause it's all illegal anyways. And you try and stop 'em . . . They'd shoot you down, sure as look at ya!"

Bill rolled his eyes and wished he was dead.

An escape from the Fountain of Hormones only to splash into a really *truly* sticky situation.

"Gee—you don't mean *Chism*, do you?" asked Bgr.

"Nope! That's Jism like I done said. What, can't hear me, boy? Ain't Ah *projectin'* right?" Alf Bob slapped his knee and wheezed with laugher. "Lord have mercy! And what I hear lately is that the dangblasted orneriest outlaw *east* of the Messasucki just signed up with the gang for a spell. You probably heard tell of him, Bill. He's yore namesake! That'd be William Boner. Alias Billy the Kidney!"

The Chinger bounced on the seat with excitement, splintering and crunching it. "Gee—this is it! This is the place."

"What the bowb are you talking about?" Bill blubbered through the bitter bite of bile on his lips.

"Once in a while, Delazny would babble about what seemed to be at the very core of the Fountain of Hormones. The paradigm of human heterosexuality. I heard him mention this Jism Gang and Billy the Kidney! Why, it all makes sense, doesn't it Bill?"

"Could you kindly shut up for awhile and let me die." Bill suggested.

"Think about it, Bill. Forget your digestive condition and think of the stars! Think of the symbolic representation of the actual energies in Flux, Trooper! The rampant assault on the female countryside by the male principle! This is where it's all happening, Bill! If I can short-circuit Frank and Jesse and Billy, the Chinger war will be over, and you humans will be warm, friendly and docile which, P.S., will be a very rare change!"

"Aren't you forgetting about Delazny? He's still sniffing about somewhere!"

"I got my trusty six-shooter, kemo sabe!" shouted the Chinger, waving his little gun excitedly. "I'll waste that bowbhead in the bargain! He tricked me and the whole Chinger Army! I'm gonna fill the varmint full of lead!"

Bill wasn't so sure about any of this. If he didn't die at once all he wanted was to get off the stagecoach. And stay as far away as he could from more violence. He had had enough.

"That's fine for you, Chinger. But if the Troopers can't find me I think maybe Irma and I will just settle down somewhere and raise porkuswine or something nice like that."

"Strange fella, talking to yourself like that," said Alf Bob. "But let me warn you. People who take on the Jism gang jest about *always* end up planted in Shoe Hill!"

"You mean, 'Boot Hill,' don't you old timer?" said Bill, remembering his ACTION WESTERN SHOOT-OUT COMIX.

"Hell, no. That's in Dodge City. What do you think I am, stupid?"

Bill apologized and strongly suggested to Bgr to keep his mouth shut as well for the duration of the journey. Maybe he could get some shut-eye and forget what was happening to his guts. But just as he was dropping off, a plaintive voice interrupted his repose.

"Bill!"

Bill opened his eyes and leaned over the side of the coach. Irma was leaning out of the window, turning a petulant frown his way.

"Yes, ma little desert flower, sweetest blossom of the prairie," Bill found himself saying. Pretty disgusting stuff. Must be Western-speak.

"I don't like it down here. It's stuffy. Can I ride up there with you?"

"Golly—I don't know, honey-bunch!"

"Your lady friend wants to ride up here? Why sure! But she'll have to sit in my lap!"

The scraggly old man wheezed with laughter.

Bill relayed the message to Irma, who decided, after all, to stay in the coach.

The sun was a fiery red ball on the purple horizon when the buildings of Mulch Gulch rode into view, snaggly poking into the air like rotting teeth in a twisted jaw. The dust in the air made sundown a bloody thing that washed the outskirts of "the Gulch" (as Alf Bob called it) with bleak and ruddy light and sepia shadows. It was a town that could have been ripped straight from Bill's Three-Dee Comix—cardboard and cheap paint and all. It smelled of horses and dust, and horseapples and open drains, and much less pleasant things, and the people that walked its dusty, muddy streets and snarled at the stagecoach as it pulled in looked haggard and mean.

Bill felt like he was back home on Phigerinadon II.

"Whooooooaaaaa!" said Alf Bob Barker, pulling on the reins just as the horses reached the Uterine Hotel. "Well, podner. This is it. We'll be a-holding up here for the night. You have ma thanks for a job well done. Them rabbits you scared away were mean varmints!" He winked cagily then turned and threw all the luggage down into the mud before jumping down to help the passengers out of the coach.

Bill jumped off as well, opened the coach door and held his arms wide and Irma dropped into them. Within moments, her own arms were tightly wrapped around Bill's back, and their lips were locked in frantic osculation.

"Oh Bill!" said Irma, panting passionately.

"Oh Irma," said Bill, opening his belt frantically.

"Not here, you foolish, passionate devil!" she laughed and pushed him away.

"Where?" Bill husked passionately.

"I know," said Irma coquettishly. "I'll just go and register at the hotel, my darling. Then I'll go and powder my nose. The hotel desk clerk will give you my room number. We'll order room service so we don't have to ever go out, ever again. We'll spend eternity there. Now, doesn't that sound like real fun?"

It sounded like the stuff that dreams are made of to Bill. But there were other temptations. A glimpse of something very interesting caught the corner of his eye. Across the way, right next to the promised Ovum Bank, was a quite interesting structure, bearing a sign that read, NEW GOON SALOON.

"Good as done, dearest one! Go—and I will see you soonest!" he gurgled, finding it difficult to speak with all the saliva gushing into his mouth.

Irma gave him a sweet peck on his cheek and then bustled into the hotel with the rest of the passengers of the stagecoach to check in.

"Come on Bgr," gargled Bill. "Let us mosey on over to that thar saloon and I'll buy you a shot of Old Overcoat!"

"Good thinking old hoss. I can't imagine a better place to reconnoiter the situation!"

They moseyed moistly through the mud and pushed through the swinging doors of the New Goon Saloon.

It was like unto a paradise to Bill! Without a doubt,

it was his kind of place. The problem with Trooper canteens, as well as most of the bars in the known universe, was that they were far too high-tech. You didn't really know where the plastic ended and the good honest booze began. No, Bill liked his bars not only soaked in atmosphere, but just plain *soaked*, and the New Goon Saloon certainly fit the bill. And the Bill.

The place was dark and roomy, awash with the smell of ancient beer, spilled whiskey and dead cigars, the sound of clinking glass, drunken conversation and melting livers. The bar—a dark mahogany affair—stretched the length of the large room, brightly shining with brass fixtures. Behind it was a huge mural of a reclining woman with bits of gauze drapery falling from her plump body. She smiled down warmly on the alcoholic scene below. The bartender—a bald-headed large-moustachioed individual with an impressive gut—was lazily polishing a glass. He looked up as they entered. He did not seem at all surprised to see a four-armed lizard wearing a western outfit hop up onto his bar.

"Name your poison, gents?" he said.

"Hydrofluoric acid on the rocks," Bill said.

"Ho-ho, sonny, yore quite a card. Quintuple bourbon in a beer mug coming up. What about your little green chum here?"

"Just a sarsaparilla for me, please," said the Chinger. "And I'll need a straw with that."

Eyes growing accustomed to the cool dimness, Bill looked around at the crowd. Men in western garb sat around tables here and there. In the corner, there was a small poker game going on.

"What a great place!" said Bill happily.

"Here you go, gents!" said the bartender, sliding their drinks down the smooth surface of the bar. "That'll be six bits."

"Gee—my friend's paying," said Bgr. He washed his hands in the sarsaparilla then ate his straw.

"Uh—how much is six bits, mister?"

"No jokes, sonny. Seventy-five cents."

"Yeah, sure." Bill turned out his pockets. All he had was lint. He took a healthy gulp of his whiskey, just in case. "Do you take Trooper Cred Fingernails here?" He held up his pinky, upon which was implanted his meager Trooper credit account.

The bartender scowled. "No funny games, cowboy. This is a cash and carry bar. Pay up. And no greenbacks. If it don't clank I don't want it."

Bill hadn't the slightest idea what the barman was talking about. He had none of those things. But maybe he could barter. Trade his gun for booze. He pulled it out.

The bartender, eyes starting with fear, shoved his hands high in the air and wiggled his fingers like crazy. "Bubbling Beezelbub buster! Don't shoot! Them drinks is on the house."

What a kind man this bartender indeed was. Bill dropped the pistol on the bar and grabbed for the glass. As the revolver struck the hard wood the cylinder popped free and bullets spilled across the bartop. The bartender poked hesitantly at the bullets and his jaw dropped. Bill glugged and the Chinger munched his straw.

"Well, hogtie my little doggies," the barman said. "This here's a silver bullet! I'll be happy to take it in trade. For a silver bullet you gentlemen can drink till you drop. But that's beside the point. If you've got silver bullets that must mean—"

The bartender looked at Bill with awe and wonder.

"Why, that must mean that you're the Stoned Ranger!"

CHAPTER 18

THE BALLAD OF
BILLY THE KIDNEY

"THE WHAT?" SAID BILL.

"The Stoned Ranger, man! I *thought* you looked familiar!" The bartender was beaming and fawning at the same time. Very difficult to do.

All heads in the bar turned their way—even the ones on the beer mugs.

"You must have heard that Billy the Kidney was coming into town with the Jism Gang!" The bartender handed the silver bullet back to Bill. "Here. I'm on your side. You better take this back. You're going to need all your bullets, big guy!"

"Stoned Ranger?" whispered Bill to Bgr. "What is he talking about?"

"Don't rock the boat, as we say in the Chinger navy,"

said Bgr. "We're getting free drinks and straws aren't we?" He jumped up onto the bar and grabbed a handful of straws and started munching them.

A man dressed in buckskins, sporting a long, dangling beard and mustaches stood up from a table and walked over to the bar, extending a welcoming hand. "Well, howdy there, partner. Been wanting to meet you for jest a bundle of years. Name's Hiccup! Wild Will Hiccup!"

"Pleased to meet you, Wild!" said Bill, feeling agreeable with all the whiskey now tucked beneath his belt and working its way irrevocably towards his already hobnailed liver, and looking forward to an endless day of free drinking ahead of him. "But I don't really know what you're talking about. My name is Bill. With two l's."

"Don't listen to him!" shouted Bgr, jumping up and down on the bar, waving his arms for attention. "He's the Stoned Ranger all right, sure enough. Just that he's a bit shy in front of strangers, admitting that he has gunned down more men than could fill an entire train. And caboose. I know all this for I am his faithful Chinger companion, Procto. Or something like that. We're here looking for deadly destiny with the Jism Gang and Billy the Kidney. And by the way, you all ain't seen a critter name of Delazny hereabouts, have you?"

Wild Will raised bushy eyebrows high. "Billy the Kidney, you say. Weeee doggies! You're gunnin' for a slippery character all right. Don't know nothin' about no Deloozknee, Stoned Ranger and Procto, but I can tell you a heap of tall tales 'bout Billy the Kidney! 'Fact, Ah happen to be not merely a biographer of the Kidney, but a bibliographer of all the ballads, legends and penny dreadfuls that have been written about the durned fella."

"Well, I guess it wouldn't hurt none to hear about the man we're after, right Bill?" said Bgr.

Bill shrugged, picked up his drink and drained it. "Just

keep the alcohol flowin', compañeros, and I'm all ears!" He smiled blearily as the glass was slammed down in front of him. Something tickled at his memory. Something? Someone? A new wave of alcohol washed away the thought and he groped for the drink. Raising it to his new friend Wild Will Hiccup, they heartily toasted one another's health.

"Doc!" cried Wild Will, cupping his hand. "Doc Shoreleave! Bring my sack from the table over here." He turned back to Bill. "Got myself a couple of new books just today 'bout the Kidney. I'll jest wet mah whistle here, and we'll have a public readin'!"

Wild Will sipped from the large whiskey glass, then gave the rest of the drink to the man who carried his bag. Doc Shoreleave had a hacking cough and dreadful bags under his eyes. "Thanks, Doc. Poor Doc. Accidentally got beamed down here from the Starship UNTERMENSCH. He and Sheriff Wyatt Slurp go way back with the Jism Gang, don't you, Doc?"

The Doc just muttered something about spocks before his eyes, slammed the rest of the triple down his throat, then went back to slump in his chair. Wild Will rummaged through his sack, pulled out two cheaply printed books with garish covers and pulpy paper. He cleared his throat, raised his hand for silence and commenced reading the first:

THE PALM IS A HAIRY MISTRESS
(being the eleventh volume in
The Putz Thru
Tomorrow series)
by
Robert A. Heiny

Denver shot its wad.

Shot great streams of rockets, trying to nuke Billy the Kidney and I, out in the desert.

But little did the hardware jockeys know it, but Billy and I were on the Moon mining ice and having our way with our line-marriages of nubile pubescents and worshipful women, they were harsh mistresses indeed!, up there with our good buddy, Shylock the hardup computer. (Lusty bucket of neuristors just didn't want *any* old piece of flesh!)

My old man, Lazarus Hung, taught me two things. "Be kind to women" and "Don't take any crap from them." So when Denver bombed our Freehold out in the desert we figured we better give them a taste of their own medicine, so we diverted a few asteroids from the space-lanes and nailed the bastards but good.

TANSTAAFL.

That means "There ain't no such thing as a free lawyer." Ask me, I know, I was known as Litigious Larry before I changed my name. I've had more lawsuits than you have had pastrami sandwiches. It's damned true. Toe-of-a-bitch!

Anyway, back to Billy.

The Kidney and I, we go way back. Sucker never does get older, don't know how he does it. I remember heading back in my time machine, the S.S. BOOTSTRAPS, and meeting him and Pat Garrett at a pleasure house in Oklahoma City. The Kidney was just a squirt then, went by the name of William Boner. Mean little sucker. Watch him gun down five men in cold blood, and I think to self, this guy's just a skin full of testosterone! We sure could use him back on the Moon!

Says, "Okay!" when I tell him about all the free sex. Don't tell him about the lawyers or the lunches, though.

Funny thing though.

Time travel ride shakes him up lots.

And hell, he mutates!

So how am I supposed to know *this* would happen. Anyway, Billy the Kidney's still a great guy and all, we just have a robo-mop trail along after him, cleaning up.

Like Lazarus Hung says, "A man gains immortality through his brain and his sexual endeavors." Sounds nice, though a little male-chauv-piggish.

The reading was interrupted by a hoarse shout from without the swinging saloon doors.

"It's the Jism Gang! They're here. And the Kidney is—"

Bang! The sound of an echoing shot was followed instantly by a *bwanng* sound as the ricochet whistled about the room.

"Arggh!" said the voice. A big man in boots and a bloody vest staggered through the swinging doors. "They got me!" He collapsed, his spurs pointing toward the ceiling, still jingling like Christmas bells.

"Oh Lordy!" said Wild Will, hastily closing his books and ducking under a table. "It's the Kidney! And he's a-comin' here! Hide, Stoned Ranger! Hide, Procto! The Kidney's a killer when he's in black spirits, and when he hears the Stoned Ranger's here, he's not gonna be in a good mood!"

Such was the air of gloom and doom projected by all the drinkers in the saloon as they dived beneath chairs and tables, that even Bgr's knees started knocking. The Chinger made a swan dive behind the bar. "Hide, Bill!" he shouted back. "I got bad vibes about this!"

Bill, who was working thirstily on his whiskey, was too plastered to really care much. He made a token effort to get behind the bar, but he found that his spurs had somehow gotten tangled with the bar rail. He was working on trying to take off his boots when the saloon door slammed open and the first of the outlaws squished through.

"It's Frank! Frank Jism!" came a frightened whisper from beneath one of the tables.

Bill was so stunned by the thing that walked in that

he stopped his struggles and simply stared.

The creature before him looked like a giant comic book thought-balloon dressed in Western garb. Its body was round, bulbous and sheened with a thick fluid. Dark eyes peered malevolently out from beneath a black hat. Around its bulbous, glistening base was a belt and a gun. But its waist trailed off into a thin whiplike flagellum, which somehow not only supported its entire body, but provided its forward movement as well.

Frank Jism was a gigantic spermatozoon!

"Eggs!" Frank Jism ejaculated. "Where are the goddamned dancing eggs, fer Chrissakes!" A protoplasmic arm and hand and finger held a gun. It squeezed off a round into the ceiling, and plaster rained down. It turned squinty little eyes toward Bill. "You, there, pardner. How *cum* you're not a-quiverin' and a-quakin' like these other cowards! How cum you're not a'hidin' underneath a table."

The sperm squished over toward Bill, a dripping frown on its liquid face.

"Care for a drink?" asked Bill.

"I don't want no goddamned drink!" Frank Jism snarled liquidly. "I wanna know how cum you think yer such a hero!"

It stuck its gun directly into one of Bill's nostrils.

The cold metal was enough to wake up Bill's heretofore intoxicated sense of self-preservation. "Well, actually, Frank, to tell you the truth, I can't move. My boot's stuck." He pointed down to the spur caught in the bar rail and wiggled his foot. For some reason, when he pulled on it again, his foot slid out, revealing a damp and noisome sock.

The reaction on Frank Jism was immediate. His pale white face turned an immediate beet red. He started choking. The gun dropped from his hands and he fell back, gasping.

Immediately, a hail of bullets erupted from beneath the tables and behind the bars, rupturing the membranous surface of the giant sperm's skin. Frank Jism collapsed upon the ground, his flagellum whipping about like a dying snake.

With a gasp, Frank Jism died.

"Geez, Stoned Ranger!" cried somebody. "Put your boot back on! You'll kill us all."

Bill slipped his sock back into his boot and then looked back at Frank Jism on the floor, melting away like an ice cube on the stove. Shuddering, he poked his nose into his glass and finished his whiskey.

"Okay!" a growling voice cried from beyond the door. "Reach for the ceiling, toadstool!"

Bill lifted his hands.

Another sperm slithered through the doorway. It looked exactly like Frank Jism, only this one had a scar running down its bulbous face and body.

"It's Jesse!" cried the others "Jesse Jism."

The sperm wiggled up to the fallen body of his brother. He kicked it once with his flagellum, and the body just oozed all the way flat.

"Who done this?" he whispered through gritted pseudo teeth.

An army of arms stabbed pointing fingers toward Bill from beneath tables. "He done it! Him! The Stoned Ranger!"

Jesse Jism wiggled back a pace. "The Stoned Ranger!?"

"The Stoned Ranger!" chorused the others.

Bill said, "I think there's a case of mistaken identity here!"

"Stoned Ranger, you kilt my brother in cold blood! Do you know who I am?"

"They say you're Jesse Jism," said Bill, slurring his words a bit. "But you look like a great big sperm to me!"

Jesse Jism grinned. "That's what I am, partner. The biggest sperm west of the Vasectomy River. And I'm the meanest one, too. So fill your hand and get ready to die quick, 'cause vengeance is mine!''

Quick as lubricated lightning, Jesse Jism pulled his gun.

In fact, the outlaw had his out before Bill even thought to go for his own weapon. The outlaw gun was pointing, and the trigger finger was just about to pull, when suddenly the Chinger burst through the front of the bar, tiny guns blazing.

Bullets tore into the front of Jesse Jism's chest, or into the spot where his chest would be if he had a chest. The outlaw dropped his gun and staggered, looking down at the gaping hole in his middle. ''Stoned Ranger! How you done that? I din't even see your gun hand *move!*''

A volley of bullets tore from the audience beneath the tables, slashing Jesse Jism the sperm into shreds and rips and tatters, flattening him into a similar flat ruin as his brother Frank.

''Whoa *wheeee!*'' cried the townspeople. ''Yay Stoned Ranger! He kilt the Jism brothers!''

Bill twisted his boot toe on the floor in mock embarrassment. And saw the Chinger Bgr standing by the hole he had knocked in the bar, blowing down the barrel of his smoking gun. ''Hey, *somebody* had to do it!''

Wild Will stepped up and slapped Bill on his back. ''Good shootin' fella! Well, the brothers are dead, but Billy the Kidney and the Jism Gang are still out there somewhere, laying low!''

A voice shouted from beyond the door. ''Frank! Jesse! You guys okay?''

''They're dead, Billy the Kidney!'' snarled the bartender. ''We got ourselves the Stoned Ranger in here, and you'll be just as dead if you waggle your tail in here!''

''Arrrgh!'' he snarled. ''Did you say the Stoned Ranger? Well, we've gotta make our deposit in the Ovum Bank tomorrow, and no Stoned Ranger is gonna stop us! Tell ya what, Stoney. I'm challengin' you to a shoot-out! Yeah, just you an' me, Billy the Kidney! At the No-Go Corral. Tomorrow, at the crack of dawn!"

"Right!" cried the bartender. "He'll be there, Billy. Just get ready for a trip to Boot Hill!"

"You mean 'Shoe Hill,' don't you," said Bill blearily.

"Naw. Billy bought himself a grave in Dodge City." cried the bartender. "Now you and your gang get your butts outta here, Billy!"

There was the sound of cursing, and then the pounding of horses' hooves clattering away out of town.

The bartender grinned back at Bill and the others. "They're gone! The Jism Gang and Billy the Kidney got run outta town! Hip hip hooray for the Stoned Ranger and his faithful companion Procto!"

"Hip hip hooray!"

Bill smiled blurrily. "Gosh, sounds good to me. Only what about his showdown at the No-Go Corral tomorrow?"

"Don't worry, Stoned Ranger!" said Wild Will, "Just so happens that the Sheriff is coming back in tonight on the ten-ten from Kansas City. He'll help you out!"

"Right!" said the Chinger. "And remember, you've got Irma waiting for you back in the hotel room! Gee— this is just great! The Ultimate Confrontation, tomorrow at dawn! This could be the very thing to nullify the Over-Gland! How symbolic!"

Bill did not hear the last part of Bgr's enthusiastic speech. He only heard the name "Irma," and that was enough.

"Irma!" he said, remembering. "And it's about time for me to head back to her waiting arms!"

"Here you go, sport!" said the bartender. "Another splash for the road, huh?" He filled Bill's glass with whiskey. "She's a-waitin' for you, hero!"

"You betcha!" cried Bill, draining the glass, turning unsteadily and started for the door and the hotel across the street.

"Enjoy yourself, Bill," the Chinger called after him.

"I'll just stay here and enjoy a straw or two and jaw some with Wild Will!"

"Shwush," said Bill, hardly noticing, staggering out toward the door.

"Irma!" he said. "IRMA!"

How he yearned for her, yearned for her eyes, yearned to whisper sweet nothings in her ears. Bill had never felt like this before, not in his entire life.

So this was it, he thought, blinking through the reddish fog of alcohol.

He was *in love*!

Sigh!

He didn't know if it was his love for Irma or the whiskey, but he felt as happy as an Altairean sandhog in rut. Life had meaning after all, and all the meaning in life had fawnlike eyes, and a sweet smile and a cute nose and was spelled I-R-M-A!

And wonder of wonders, she loved him too!

Galactic Troopers didn't fall in love. There were specific regulations forbidding it. But Bill didn't care, mad, headstrong fool that he was. Could he finally, after all this time, feel something stirring in this boot-camp hardened heart? Sweet, gentle emotion!

Ah, sweet dear Irma!

With a lilt in his step, a song in his heart, alcohol in his brain and cirrhosis at the doorstep, Bill stumbled up the steps to the hotel. The clerk in the lobby was only too happy to tell Bill that Miss Irma had checked into Room 122, and that she was expecting him, apparently, having just ordered up two bottles of champagne and a rare sirloin steak from Room Service.

Bill grinned sappily.

His heart beating out the rhythm of his passion, Bill stumbled down the hallway, looking for the room.

Eventually, the numbers "1-2-2" reared up before his fevered eyes. He tried the door. It was locked.

He knocked.

There was no answer.

But what was that? Bill thought he heard sighs of passion from within.

"Irma, my shweet!" he called out throatily. "It is I, Bill, your beloved. Let me in, darling."

There was the sound of sudden screams and breaking furniture. Bill's head pounded with alarm.

Was something violent going on in there?

Irma was in trouble.

"Don't worry, Irma!" Bill called. "I'll save you."

He backed up, ran forward and aimed a great Camp Leon Trotsky-trained shoulder at the wood. One slam, that was all it took, and Bill crashed through the flimsy door. He staggered into the darkened room, bellowing, "Irma! Irma! Where are you! Irma!"

He immediately slipped on the empty champagne bottle and crashed face first to the floor.

He blinked blearily up from his sprawl on the ground, only to find two faces staring back at him, poking out of the covers of the big brass bed.

One belonged to Irma.

The other face in the bed belonged to the evil Dr. Latex Delazny!

CHAPTER 19

SHOOTOUT AT THE NO-GO CORRAL

"IRMA!" CRIED BILL. HE BLINKED HIS EYES, bulged and popped them in astonishment at the sight before him: his darling, the love of his life, under the sheets with his worst enemy, a villain intent upon rule of the universe.

"Irma! I'm here to save you!"

He hurled himself forward—then squealed to a stop and Irma called out.

"Stow it, buster," she snarled, training a derringer on him. "You harm a single hair on my darling's balding skull and I'll put a slug of lead right through your pinhead where, theory has it, you're supposed to have a brain."

"But—but—" stammered Bill. Reluctantly putting

one and one together to get a horrifying two. Slowly but inescapably, reluctantly, the horrible truth trickled through into his consciousness and down between the alcohol loaded synapses.

"This can't be true! You're *my* girl!" Bill croaked helplessly.

"Men! A gal says a few silly words, and you think you own her! Real life just ain't like that, buster. You've been reading too many romance comics. Now split." She sneered at him with contempt.

"But I *love* you, Irma," he whined in sickening self-pity. "And you said you *loved* me!"

"So I'm fickle. It's a woman's prerogative to change her mind." She snuggled up to Delazny, nibbled on his shell-like ear. Clam shell, that is. "I have found myself a *real* man!"

"But your father—he said that while Delazny lusted after you, you always spurned him! That was one of the reasons that good man went ga-ga!" He turned to Delazny. "Irma was one of the reasons you wanted to plumb the secrets of the Over-Gland! That must be it! You're here, you discovered the secret power of attraction that drives women out of their mind, beyond reason."

"Actually, no, not quite yet," said Delazny. "Sorry, old sport . . . that happens tomorrow when Billy the Kidney, the Jism Gang and I finish you and the opposition at the No-Go Corral and then plunder the outlaw savings at the Ovum Bank. You see, the secrets of universal power reside there." He looked at Irma and smiled. "Irma and I just ran into each other in the lobby and we hit it off at once."

"I realized how much I'd missed him. I was so naive, so priggish back in the old days. So, if you don't mind old friend, and I do mean *old*, why don't you split."

"And," Delazny sneered, "May I add my recommendation to that, pardner. Get lost. I'll see you tomorrow at sun-up! Just make sure you order yourself up a nice coffin!"

"Irma!" said Bill, feeling his vulnerable heart melting in his chest and slowly dripping down to his heels. "What's wrong with *me*!"

Irma curled a disdainful lip. "Well, those fangs for one thing."

"You said you *liked* my fangs!"

"You just don't know how to treat a girl, Bill," sighed Irma with disdain.

"I can learn! Irma . . . please . . . give me another chance! Don't stay with this villain. Come away with me now!" Bill fell to his knees, begging, acting the complete idiot.

"Go, Bill. For my new love is absolutely *mythic*!"

Bill's head was whirling, and there was only an ache in his chest now where his heart should have been. He turned and staggered shaken from the room, having severe difficulty breathing.

Dr. Delazny!

Dr. Delazny and *Irma*!

Life, which never was exactly a bed of roses, was getting a little too awful of late. Bill had never expected justice. But it would have been nice to have some. He sighed deeply as he stumbled down the stairs.

No justice. Just bribery, chicanery and the old boys network. And booze. He hurried back towards the saloon before the others got too far ahead of him.

The horizon was like a cracked egg, and dawn resembled its yellow yolk as sticky albumen was spreading now over the distant mountain and desert. The smell of death was already in the air. The morning tasted of boots and graves and the cold, arid desert. Bill's spurs jingled as he walked toward the place they called the No-Go Corral, his holster unfastened, fresh bullets in his revolver, the Chinger who once was Eager Beager strolling at his side.

"Gee—I hope that you are ready, Bill?"

"I reckon," said Bill.

"This is shore a red-letter day in the history of the Universe!"

"Yep."

"How you feeling?"

"Murderous and rotten."

"Now that is what I call real great, Bill. Just great. Nothing like lots of violence to bring peace to the galaxy, huh?"

A hangover the size of the Grand Canyon fissured through Bill's head. His mouth felt like Death Valley filled with flies and then sauteed. His stomach resembled the fermenting vat in the Galactic Glueworks. His liver, if he could see it, which he did not want to, must look as though the Great Railway Line had been spiked into it with twenty pound sledgehammers.

Yep. Last night he'd tromped himself over to the Saloon and taken the bartender up on the offer of unlimited free drinks, letting the other cowpokes and gamblers and pimps have a few sips here and there, in return for their heartfelt commiseration over his misfortune. The Chinger had disappeared sometime during the night, but Wild Will and Doc Shoreleave were still there, and they gladly accepted the hero's hospitality, giving him sympathy for the loss of Irma, and telling him their own stories of lost loves, betrayals, sadnesses and heroic binges.

Doc Shoreleave was a particular treasure trove, since his tastes ran toward the alien and the exotic, and had afforded him plenty of opportunity for odd heartbreak. At the moment, for example, he was recovering from the stress of a particularly torrid affair he had had with the science officer of his last ship, the U.S.S. CENTERPIECE, a half-human, half-Metalloid sadist with even more perverted tastes than his. The Doc had even tried to drop his drawers and show them his scars that the passionate affair had left him with. But that was too much for even this hard-bitten crew and they had run him out of town and settled back for more drinking.

At about ten-thirty, the Sheriff, Wyatt Slurp, had joined them as promised, making up for lost time by helping them all drink the bar dry.

Bill had passed out sometime after midnight, lying on the bar with his feet propped on the Doc's face and his head pillowed on a bottle of Old Sewagemaster whiskey. He'd woken up to the sound of the Chinger ex-Eager Beager screeching in his ear about it being almost dawn. The only thing that got him up was Trooper reflexes. But once he got going, the thought of facing off with Dr. Delazny and filling the bastard full of hot lead (or rather, in his case, hot silver) gave him just the motivation he needed to bear up under his crashing hangover.

"Gee—" The Chinger had said when he told him about the events in the hotel room last night. "Too bad, Bill. But remember, there are plenty more kraxels to pringle, as we Chingers so aptly say!"

Oh well, who would expect a *Chinger* to understand the pain and heartache of a lost love? Particularly one who pringled kraxels. Yet the little alien glommed onto the fact that Bill wanted to waste Dr. Delazny, and milked it for all he was worth.

"Gee, Bill! I bet there's a big, satisfied smile on that Delazny's face!" he said now as Bill marched toward the No-Go Corral, with Wild Will, Doc Shoreleave and Wyatt Slurp as backup.

"Shut up, Chinger!" Bill sufflated.

"Shouldn't egg on a man going into a shootout like that, ought to let him relax," said Wyatt Slurp, combing his long mustaches. Two bright polished Colt .45s rode in his gunbelt. And his boots were shined to a bright finish, as were all the boots of the gun party—courtesy of the Chinger ex-Eager Beager who didn't need sleep and got a whiff of nostalgia from this function that he hadn't had in years.

"I'm relaxin' fine, thanks!" said Doc Shoreleave, glugging down a swallow of whiskey. He passed the bottle to Bill, who refused.

"Nope," said Bill, his eyes squinting down against the brightening horizon. "I want my senses raw and sharp and mean when I get Delazny in my gun sights."

"That's the old fighting spirit, Bill!" said the Chinger, raising up four clenched reptilian paws. "That's the way we'll defeat Delazny and Billy the Kidney and his gang! Just like we finished off the Jism brothers last night!"

Bill spat into the dust. "Yeah!"

The tops of the buildings comprising the No-Go Corral hove into view ahead. The stables and the outbuildings were surrounded by a wooden fence. In front of this fence stood a solitary man, surrounded by the ugliest bunch of spermatozoa that Bill had ever seen.

"Step aside, Bill!" called Dr. Latex Delazny. The mad scientist was dressed entirely in black, except for the silvery revolvers riding on his hips, ready for action. "We're headed for the Ovum Bank to make the Withdrawal of the Century! No! The Withdrawal of all Eternity! Right, boys?"

"Right, Doctor D.!" chorused the twenty or so sperm stationed all around him, balancing on their thin flagella just as the James Brothers had.

"It's bang, bang, bang, and the universe is mine!" cried Doctor Delazny. "And, Bill, Irma asked me to say Hi! to you."

"You just made that up now!" said Bill, reaching for his six-gun.

Wyatt Slurp stopped him. "No, Bill. Wait until they draw first 'cause that's the way we guys in the white hats play it."

They took a few more steps forward, then stopped short as Dr. Delazny held up a halting hand. "Wait a moment, folks. I want to take this brief opportunity before we blow you all away to introduce you to a very good pal of mine, Mr. Billy the Kidney!" Delazny looked behind him. "Why don't you step on out and take a bow, Billy!"

A particularly warped and dirty sperm wearing tattered clothes and a bullet-holed hat squiggled out and stared at his opponents with eyes that had less life than a dead fish. The Kidney was chawing something in his mouth, and a bulge worked around its body like an animated carbuncle.

Billy the Kidney spat out a gob of tobacco juice that clanged onto the hard-packed dirt, bounced and spattered into a fence post.

"Ya varmints wanna fight, huh? Ya think ya can kill my friends the Jism Brothers and get away with it? Well, get ready to get turned to vulture chow and look forward to eternity in Shoe Hill." He drew his guns, twirled them fancily, then pointed them into the air. "And guess who's coming to dinner!"

Bill looked up. Hovering over the scene was a bunch of particularly ugly buzzards, looking down upon the good guys and licking their beaky chops.

"Don't kid me Kidney," said Wyatt Slurp. "You've spat your last spit. Since you've got a little help in your little argument with Bill here, me and the Doc are gonna settle our runnin' account with you, right this mornin'. 'Sides, it'd be a nice change if we can prevent you boys from havin' your way with the Bank!"

Delazny laughed. "That's what you think, Sheriff. I forgot to mention to you, that I have also enlisted the services of the entire Vindaloo Indian Nation in this little gunfight!" He waved his free hand. "Come on out, boys, and show yourselves!"

From behind the stables squirmed at least fifty more spermatozoa, wearing feathers, loincloths and single moccasins on their flagella. Each held a bow and arrow, and all of these were aimed at Bill and Company.

Bill's eyes widened. With good reason. Not only the threat to his life but it isn't every day you run across giant red Indian spermatozoa.

Unhappily he had a fine view of the hills, down which coursed a stream of thousands upon thousands of Vindaloo Indians, glistening wetly in the rising sun.

"I guess that's one nice thing about working with sperm!" said Dr. Delazny. "Where you find one, there's a couple of million more just hanging around!"

"Gee, guys," said the Bgr the Chinger. "It doesn't look good does it!"

Doc Shoreleave shook his head sadly, shrugging. "Hell, I guess that's what life's all about, though, isn't it. Staring us right in our faces. It's the never-ending, striving, yearning, heaving indefinable *urge* to *merge*. That's what Nature wants! And what is Nature but a great cosmic pursuit of yang by yin! Individuality? The human *soul*? Bah! It means nothing compared to the heaving sea of mindless, salivating critters of procreation that govern the depths of human being!" He gestured out to the sea of spermy outlaws and Indians, coughed, and then drew his six-shooters. "Our destiny gentlemen! Let us not go out gracefully!"

"Well, Bill," the Chinger said ruminatively, "I think I was rather foolish to even think I could stop *this* phenomenon!" Eager Beager's tail swished around and he touched it to his mouth, ceremoniously.

"What's that?" asked Bill, trying to recover his nerve and not quite succeeding. "A Chinger religious ritual?"

"Not quite, Bill. I'm just kissing my tail good-bye!"

A war-whoop rose up from the assembled Indians. They started to slide down the hills, waving spears and chanting. They were savage-looking sperm, no question, done up in warpaint, looking, fierce and mean as a group of Galilean gophers on Galactic Ground Hog day.

"Shee—eet," said Wyatt Slurp. "This morning's going to make the Little Big Horn look like Custer's Last Ice Cream Stand!" He raised his gun and aimed. "Well, if we're gonna die—we might as well die like men!" He plugged a Jism Gang member right between the vacuoles.

"But I'm not a man!" observed Bgr. "I'm a Chinger! I really don't think I should be here."

"Tough titty, reptile," said Doc Shoreleave as the bullets and arrows started whizzing past their ears. "Get those guns going!" His own weapons started blazing and a row of the nearest Indians bit the dust messily.

Eager Beager hastily jumped behind a rock, from which he blasted away at their multitude of attackers.

As the first arrows flew any vestige of his Western manliness suddenly fled from Bill. This was no fight, this was a massacre. The only reasonable thing any one with a grain of intelligence should do was *vamoose*!

However, when Bill turned to run, he saw that he was cut off at the pass. An enormous quantity of Vindaloo Indians had flowed behind them.

They were surrounded!

"Bowb!" commented Bill intelligently as he started blasting away, hoping to shoot his way out, exploding Red-membranes willy-nilly. But for every Indian he blasted, another took its place. And he was running out of ammunition.

They were *all* running out of ammunition!

Wyatt Slurp had an arrow through his arm and a bullet in his belly, but he just kept on firing. "Sheee—eet," he laughed. "Ah only got one bullet left!" Streaming blood, he snarled out to the outlaws, "Billy! This one has your name on it!" With a war-whoop that sounded like a troop's worth of rebel yells, Sheriff Slurp charged toward the blazing group of outlaws. Splat splat spat! went the bullets as they tore into his manly body. But the Sheriff just kept on walking, though soaked in blood, until he was within spitting distance of Billy the Kidney.

"Kidney," he gasped. "Suck on this!"

Billy the Kidney turned to run, but Sheriff Slurp's bullet caught him in the back. The Kidney exploded like a water-filled balloon, and slapped hard onto the ground.

"I can die happy now!" groaned the Sheriff.

"We'll help you along!" cried the Jism Gang, who immediately filled the Sheriff so full of lead that gravity instantly dragged him down. But the firing continued until Sheriff Wyatt Slurp was finally and truly dead.

This was too much for Doc Shoreleave. He simply cracked.

"Beam me up, Beagle!" he cried to the skies. "Beam me up!"

Arrows whistled through the air, pin-cushioning him, making him look like a walking hairbrush. Or rather a standing one. He really was dead on his feet—so bristled with arrows all around him that even though he was quite dead, he couldn't fall down; he was propped up by arrows.

Bill blasted, reloaded, and blasted some more until the hammer clicked on an empty chamber and there were no more silver bullets to be had.

Somehow, through the unknown manifest workings of destiny, or stupid luck, Bill so far had escaped without a wound. But the way the volleys were flying, he knew he was going to catch some any second.

He was going to die. Croak. Expire. Bite the big one, go out for a Burton, snuff it, buy the farm, take the Black Hole Express. His life passed before his eyes. Though he been remiss of late, since he was four years old, and had not gone to church, he nurtured the secret and irrational hope that soon he would be dropping through the great Tunnel of Light within moments, and that his Great-Grandfather Bill would be waiting for him with his good old Robomule, Rusty, just a-rarin' to start plowing the heavenly sod.

An explosion cracked the sky.

"I'm coming, Great-Grandad!" cried Bill. "I'm coming *home*!"

Closing his eyes, he braced himself.

Trying not to whimper, he readied himself for Death's sting.

But Death did not sting.

In fact, the bullets stopped whizzing and the arrows stopped whistling.

"Gee! Bill, look at *that*!"

Bill opened his eyes. Bgr the Chinger was jumping up and down, pointing up at the sky excitedly.

Bill looked up.

The rocket ship was coming down on a sun-bright plume of fire, silvery and needle-shaped. Bill shielded his eyes and studied the starship more closely.

Could it be! Yes, it was!

There it was, proudly printed on the side: the name!

It was the starship called DESIRE.

It was Rick the Supernal Hero's spaceship!

The reaction amongst the Indians was fear and mass panic. As one they thundered back to the slopes of the hills, where they watched with awe as the ship settled down on the field where they had once swarmed, frying the fallen of their number. Gray spumes of smoke and yellow tongues of flame whipped and fluttered and then slowly dissipated.

"Curses!" cried Dr. Latex Delazny. "What's going on here! Modern technology is *not* supposed to work here in the Over-Gland!"

A voice erupted from the fabulous starship's outside speaker system. "Whoever said this boat was *modern*, Delazny? This ship's straight from the 1940's AMAZING STORIES!"

Bill recognized the voice. It was Rick! The *real* Rick, not the android that Delazny had created to spy upon them. The Rick for whom Bill had been first mate!

"He didn't forget me!" cried Bill. "He's come to our rescue! Yeah, Rick! Yeah!"

Delazny turned back to the hundreds of thousands of Indian hordes. "Don't worry, great Indian nation! Not even a starship and Rick the Supernal Hero can stop your massive hordes! Look how thin and flimsy the ship is! Why, you can simply fire a few tens of thousands of arrows *en masse* and it will simply tip over!"

"That's what you think, Doctor D!" said Rick through the speakers.

Then, the most astonishing thing happened!

CHAPTER 20

BILL'S BIG BANG THEORY

BILL HAD SEEN SOME INCREDIBLE THINGS IN his life. The Palace Gardens of Helior! The death-tangled Jungles of Veneria! The majestic Fertilizer Mountains of Phigerinadon II!

However, this sight unfolding now before his eyes really took the concrete cupcake.

From the top of the starship emerged a cannon, and from this cannon an explosion exploded. A wobbling globule of liquid shot up into the air over the Indian nation of the Vindaloo—a giant drop that began to slow down, undulate, and then expand and grow. It spun out like a gigantic soap bubble. It splashed down over the entirety of the Vindaloo tribes, and the Jism Gang to boot.

"What's happening?!" cried Bill.

"Arrrrr!" said Rick's voice from the speakers. "This is what they never expected—but I did. I went straight to the manufacturers and filled all the spare fuel tanks with NoPreg—the most effective spermicide in the known universe!"

And thus they died. Thus was the greatest threat removed at last. Bill heaved a great sigh of relief; all thoughts of heavenly sanctuary vanished and he looked forward to a long and full life. Unhappily still in the Troopers.

For Doctor Delazny's part, he was simply standing alone now, bereft of his army, quivering and shaking with frustration and anger. Bill strode up to him.

"Answer one question, quack, before I kill you. What did you do to my dearest Irma to make her boot me out? How could a repulsive ugly like you ever replace me in her affection?"

Bill added a certain attention-getting to his question by seizing Delazny by the throat and shaking him up and down strenuously.

"Glug!" Delazny gasped, and Bill loosened his grip. "It is the p-p-power of the Over-Gland!" he gurgled. "I admit I lied a teensy bit to you both last night. It was within my grasp. I used it on her. Its energies are irresistible."

Bill nodded. He felt a little better now. Not much, really, but it would have to do. He supposed he could find some way to forgive Irma now. He knew he still loved her. Possibly.

"Where *is* Irma, Delazny?" Another quick shake to drive home the point.

"S . . . s . . . still back in the hotel room, like I said."

"Then that's it Doc. Finito for you. You're outnumbered and have two seconds to surrender before I choke you to death. One—"

"Glug! Surrender! Fins!"

"I sort of wished you hadn't," Bill mused, throttling a bit more for his own pleasure. "It would have felt real good to kill you. Oh well . . ." He threw Delazny to the ground. "Now that your plans for galactic domination are through, and before I throttle you some more, do you think you'd have time to take a look at this bum foot of mine? After all, that *is* one of your specialties, isn't it?"

"Oh y . . . y . . . yes. The mood foot. Which one was it again, Bill?" said Delazny, eager to please. He frowned. "It looks pretty permanent. I'm not sure that there is much I can do. . . ."

Bill howled with unbridled anger, throttled the Doc again, then hurled his unconscious form away in disgust.

"Arrrrrrr! Nice choking, Bill," said Rick the Supernal Hero, climbing down the ladder. "If you don't mind I would like to get in a couple shots myself! The nerve of that guy, imprisoning me and then copying this beautiful mug onto an android!" Rick tromped over to the unconscious Dr. Delazny and rearranged a few teeth with a muddy boot. "There, that's good enough. Too bad he didn't feel it—but he will when he wakes up in my brig!" Rick patted Bill on the back. "Arrrr! Good to see you again, first mate. By the way, I want to show you something!" Around Rick's neck was slung a leather bag. From this bag he pulled a six pack of cans. He pulled one out of the plastic carrier and handed it to Bill.

Bill looked at the can. "HOLY GRAIL ALE," he elated. "Rick! You found it!"

"Arrrr! You bet matey!"

"But where?"

Rick pointed a handsome, slender finger past the rainbow that had just formed in the sky and was smiling down colorfully at them. "You're not going to believe this, Bill! But it looks like Dr. Delazny wasn't totally correct on the Over-Gland theory. You see, it's much more than that! And it's right over there!"

Bill didn't wait for an explanation. He did what it was natural for all good Troopers to do with a tall cool one in his hand: he popped the top and drained the can in one great, enjoyable, heavenly insufflation.

The fluid washed down his throat like a gentle zephyr of spring. Hops hopped gaily in their milk of liquid kindness, splashing down into his stomach where they spread gentle mists of calm and well-being throughout his body. Bill's hangover was shooed away in an instant, and the quiet joy of tasty, beery inebriation took its place. Ah, heaven!

"Yow!" he said, light filling his eyes. "This is the best beer I ever had!"

"Naturally! It's Holy Grail Ale, Bill."

"You speak in riddles, human. Clarification requested. What place do you speak of?"

"Why, the place where I got this six-pack, of course, little fella—and by the way, thanks for unlocking my cell when you found out that Delazny was a traitor to your cause. Yes—somewhere, out in the misty lands of the Over-Gland, past the angst-ridden halls of the Ego and Id, the arching columns of the Collective Unconscious, to say nothing of Dreamland, Oz and Atlantis, there lies a land far more significant than all of them!"

"What is it?" cried Bill.

"It's dreamland come true! It's everything you ever wanted but were afraid to ask for! It's the Human Over-Brewery! What urge do you think made mankind brew the first hop, distill the first corn mash? The urge for Over-inebriation, of course." Rick the Supernal Hero sighed and put a brotherly arm across Bill's back. "Ah, Bill! The very air there is poetry! Breweries and distilleries like mushrooms! And each one has its own bar!"

"Can we go, Rick?" hushed Bill breathlessly. "Can we?"

"Why, of course we can Bill! I'll take us all!"

"Gee—maybe that's the key to peace," theorized Bgr. "If all you humans were drunk all the time, which seems to be the ambition of all the ones I have met, they wouldn't be able to make war on us Chingers!"

"That's the spirit, little guy!" said Rick, taking out a can and setting it down for the Chinger. "Have a sip. Maybe you'll like it." He handed another can to Bill and burped.

Bill sipped the new brew and sighed. So good . . . so very good! He had to share this with his love. . . .

"Bill?" called a sweet voice querulously.

Bill lowered his can of Holy Grail Ale.

"Irma?"

Sure enough, looking pretty as a picture, if a little groggy, Irma Krankenhaus was walking their way.

"Bill! It's a spaceship! Are we saved Bill?" She was wearing only a nightgown, and her untied hair spilled down over her pretty face most fetchingly.

"We sure are, darling! It's my buddy, Rick, the Supernal Hero. Come to take us away from here to a far, far better place!"

"Mall World—where I can shop forever?"

"Hi, Irma. I'm Rick. Nice to meet you." Rick shook her hand amiably. Irma blinked at him for a moment.

"Oh yes . . . the one that Delazny modeled the android after. He didn't do you justice."

"Arrrrr, shucks, ma'am. Thanks."

Irma looked at Bill again.

"Bill, what happened last night? I don't remember." She didn't remember?

But of course she didn't remember! His sweet, loving Irma would never betray him while she was in her right mind. It was that bastard Delazny's total control over her endocrine glands that had caused the trouble. Bill thought quickly, lied fetchingly.

"You must have been real tired, dearest Irma! You went to bed early and switched off like a light. You slept so blissfully I did not dare awaken you," he said, falling instantly into ROMANCE KOMIX prose.

She sighed a happy sigh and Rick yipped.

"Well, let's make a toast to your happiness, mate, and then hightail it to the Over-Brewery. There's a new vat of bitter due about now, and the drinkers there tell me it's the absolutely tip top of the season."

"You'll take us back home afterwards, though, right, Rick?" said Irma.

"Sure, kid. Anything you want. C'mon Chinger. Let's load the Doc on the DESIRE. He's got a truly mythic debt to pay society."

"Gee—and when you're through with him, can we Chingers have a go at him?"

They hauled the Doctor up the ladder to the starship, managing to only drop him once or twice in the process.

Bill felt truly good. He finished the last of his second beer, crushed the can in his mighty fist, and felt even better.

"Come on up, folks," said Rick, beckoning them to climb the ladder.

Could it be, thought Bill joyously and half in the bag. Could there actually be a happy end in store for him? He, Bill a simple Trooper from Phigerinadon II, usually positioned below the sewer outlet of the galaxy. Unbelievable!

"Bill," said Irma, starting to climb the ladder. "What did you say that young man's name was?"

"Rick," said Bill, happily beaming up at her as she climbed the ladder.

She looked down at him, a curious light in her eyes. "He seems like a really nice gentleman."

"The best, Irma!" said Bill. "Rick's the best buddy a guy can have!"

Gosh, thought Bill as he followed Irma into the starship named DESIRE, ready for new thrills and adventure, to say nothing of trying to stay out of the arms of the Troopers in order to enjoy a more interesting life of rapturous love and drink and permanently goofing off duty.

Life wasn't so bad after all!

EPILOGUE

BACK OFF THE SADDLE AGAIN

"NICE FOOT YOU GOT THERE, BUDDY," SAID the bartender. "Same again?"

"Yeah," mumbled Bill.

"You're gonna have to sit up to drink it, pal. That's the canteen's rules, I'm afraid. If you can't sit up straight, we can't serve you."

"Oh," said Bill. "Yeah, sure."

The bar was a regulation lower-ranks canteen with plastiwood bar, neo-outhouse decor and a brace of beer taps, neither of which worked. In dark corners zonked Troopers slept the sleep of alcoholic bliss, escaped from the military until they reluctantly sobered up. A jittering, malfunctioning robo-mop slipped and slid and scurried about the off-yellow linoleum floor, mopping up spilled drinks and Fakey-Potato-Drips packages, cigar butts and anything, including shoes and caps, that got in the way of its inhaling nozzles.

The canteen was called "The Kill-Cat Club" because of the trophies of stuffed cats decorating its bar and its walls. Bill would have taken the turbo-tunnel into town, but the bars were even worse there—a horrifying thought!—and besides he was running out of money. And he had something important to do early tomorrow, but for the life of him he couldn't remember what the bowb it was.

He looked up blearily, trying to recall, as the robo-mop wetly slapped his face with its greasy cleaning attachment.

No wonder the bartender was admiring his foot! It had been propped up on the bar edge, while Bill had been lying firmly on the floor where he'd passed out a few moments before. Bill managed to rearrange himself, putting his head where his foot had been, and placing the latter back on the floor. It was still a cloven hoof, but Bill didn't care so much about that anymore.

Bill didn't care about anything.

When Bill was situated properly, weaving only a little, the satisfied bartender upended the bottle of Olde Paint Remover and Worm-Killer into Bill's shot glass, filling it to the brim.

Bill drank it.

It sure wasn't Holy Grail Ale, but hell, alcohol was alcohol.

Oblivion was oblivion.

"And I like your fangs, too," said the bartender, a non-com it was revealed by the stripes stitched poorly onto his wrists. Probably worked the bar for extra creds. "You're the acting DI, aren't you?"

Bill grunted.

"There's a new shipment of recruits comin' in about right now! You must be the one who will work them over?"

Bill grunted again, a pig imitation he usually enjoyed. So that's what he was doing tomorrow. He pushed his shot glass out for another drink.

"Say, aren't you drinking a little too much if you have to get up at four in the morning?" the bartender pointed out.

"Puts me in the proper sadistic mood. Fill the glass and shut up," he smiled.

The bartender shrugged. "Here you go, pal. This one's on the house. You look like you just lost your woman to your best buddy!"

Bill's eyes shot wide. The shot-glass spilled as he leaned over, grabbed the man by his shirt and pulled him halfway across the bar. "What? Does every bowbing Trooper know?"

"Gasp!" the barman gasped, slowly expiring. Bill's grasp loosened a bit and he sucked in reviving, though foul, air. "Stop! I don't know diddly-bowb about you! Sorry, I must have hit the nail on the head! Look, be my guest, keep the whole bottle!"

Bill grunted and let the guy go. "Her name was Irma. And she was the nova in my galaxy!" He shook his head and poured the whiskey and just stared at it for a moment. "But all good things pass and the end of a lovelorn Trooper is always a tragedy. She left me, Rick, it was Dumpsville for good old Bill, bad-karma gravity-hole of the universe!"

"Gee, Bill. Sorry to hear about it!"

The "Gee" earned the bartender serious scrutiny by Bill. No, there was no seam on his head, so he wasn't a disguised Chinger. Besides, Bgr the Chinger had stolen a lifeboat and escaped not long after they'd dimension-jumped out of the Over-Gland. They never *had* found the fabled Over-Brewery, either. But they had drunk all the booze in the ship, which, by hindsight, had been Bill's downfall. Rick had found Irma more attractive than the booze, which certainly must have endeared her more to him than the unconscious and sozzled Bill. At least he guessed that's what had happened.

All he knew was that he had woken up back on Colostomy IV, a note of regret pinned to his tunic and the MP's just approaching with houndlike bays of success.

And that, as the obvious but oft repeated aphorism stated, was that. There was a shortage of Drill Instructors; the last one had been eaten alive by the recruits. So they shipped him here to Camp Brezhnev, double-time, to grind the new recruits through the boot camp meat grinder and kill off the chaff.

He couldn't help now but remember, as he killed what few remaining bacteria were left in his stomach with another swig of Olde Paint Remover, what Bgr the Chinger had said in his note that Bill had found stuffed in his ear the morning after the little guy had split.

"Sorry about the misadventures and such and any trouble I might have caused by tying up with that fruit-cake of a doctor. All I wanted was a kinder, gentler universe. As, I assume, do we all, with the exception of the military. Signed Your Chinger pal, Bgr."

What bowb.

"The Chingers are our enemies!" he mouthed incoherently at the bartender.

"Yeah, pal. They sure are."

"Loose lips sink drips!"

"Right. Maybe I'd better take that bottle back now, huh?"

Bill grabbed the bottle and snarled.

The bartender backed off.

"There ain't no justice," Bill whined.

"So don't expect any."

"You're right." Bill looked down at his mood foot, sighed and belched. And reached for his glass. He raised it, started to drain it—and stopped. Something was wrong. Or right. But what? He tiptoed sluggishly through his brain cells trying to find the answer.

Foot.

Foot what?

Foot, mine.

"Foot!" he cried aloud and blinked down at his mood foot. The cloven hoof.

Cloven no more! Where the hairy thing had been was now a good solid Trooper's boot that matched exactly the one on his other foot. The foot had caught his mood!

He had given up. There was no escape. He was back in the Troopers for good, doomed to bash the barracks square forever. And his mood foot had caught that mood and provided the foot to fit the man.

Or had it? Horrified he looked back at his foot and saw the boot. But, surely, ha–ha—it was one more GI boot—and was there a foot inside. Wasn't there? But maybe he was doomed forever to have a boot instead of a foot. Which would sure look funny when he took a shower, and would play hell with his love life.

He reached down to open the boot and his horrified fingers trembled and stopped.

No! He had to find out. Whatever was stuck to the end of his leg, he had to know.

He reached down and tugged.

RETURN TO AMBER...

THE ONE *REAL* WORLD, OF WHICH ALL OTHERS, INCLUDING EARTH, ARE BUT SHADOWS

ROGER ZELAZNY

The New Amber Novel

KNIGHT OF SHADOWS   75501-7/$3.95 US/$4.95 Can

Merlin is forced to choose to ally himself with the Pattern of Amber or of Chaos. A child of both worlds, this crucial decision will decide his fate and the fate of the true world.

SIGN OF CHAOS   89637-0/$3.50 US/$4.50 Can

Merlin embarks on another marathon adventure, leading him back to the court of Amber and a final confrontation at the Keep of the Four Worlds.

The Classic Amber Series

NINE PRINCES IN AMBER 01430-0/$3.50 US/$4.50 Can
THE GUNS OF AVALON 00083-0/$3.50 US/$4.50 Can
SIGN OF THE UNICORN 00031-9/$3.50 US/$4.25 Can
THE HAND OF OBERON 01664-8/$3.50 US/$4.50 Can
THE COURTS OF CHAOS 47175-2/$3.50 US/$4.25 Can
BLOOD OF AMBER 89636-2/$3.95 US/$4.95 Can
TRUMPS OF DOOM 89635-4/$3.50 US/$3.95 Can

ARTHUR C. CLARKE'S VENUS PRIME

by Paul Preuss

VOLUME 1: BREAKING STRAIN   75344-8/$3.95 US/$4.95 CAN
Her code name is Sparta. Her beauty veils a mysterious past and abilities of superhuman dimension, the product of advanced biotechnology.

VOLUME 2: MAELSTROM   75345-6/$3.95 US/$4.95 CAN
When a team of scientists is trapped in the gaseous inferno of Venus, Sparta must risk her life to save them.

VOLUME 3: HIDE AND SEEK   75346-4/$3.95 US/$4.95 CAN
When the theft of an alien artifact, evidence of extraterrestrial life, leads to two murders, Sparta must risk her life and identity to solve the case.

VOLUME 4: THE MEDUSA ENCOUNTER
75348-0/$3.95 US/$4.95 CAN
Sparta's recovery from her last mission is interrupted as she sets out on an interplanetary investigation of her host, the Space Board.

VOLUME 5: THE DIAMOND MOON
75349-9/$3.95 US/$4.95 CAN
Sparta's mission is to monitor the exploration of Jupiter's moon, Amalthea, by the renowned Professor J.Q.R. Forester.

Each volume features a special technical infopak, including blueprints of the structures of *Venus Prime*